The Upsic
Gir

Also by Ian Strachan

The Boy in the Bubble

The Flawed Glass

Journey of 1000 Miles

Pebble on the Beach

The Second Step

throwaways

Wayne Loves Custard?

IAN STRACHAN

The Upside Down World of Ginger Nutt

To Paul,

Very best wishes,

Ian Strachan.

MAMMOTH

First published in Great Britain 1992
by Methuen Children's Books Ltd
Published 1993 by Mammoth
an imprint of Reed Consumer Books Ltd
Michelin House, 81 Fulham Road, London SW3 6RB
and Auckland, Melbourne, Singapore and Toronto

ISBN 0 7497 1474 3

A CIP catalogue record for this title
is available from the British Library

Printed and bound in Great Britain
by Cox & Wyman Ltd, Reading, Berkshire

Contents

1

A smashing time!

Ginger's nose, red from the cold on a winter's morning, was flattened against the darkened window of Mr Cumpsty's second-hand shop. To some the shop might have appeared rather sad, stuffed with people's cast-offs, but for Ginger it was a treasure cave.

The shop was on his way home after his paper round and he never failed to stop. Everything he'd ever wanted was hidden somewhere in that window, like prizes waiting to be won on a tombola.

Concealed amongst the Black and Decker drills, second-hand clothes and rusty gardening implements were roller-boots, electric trains and skateboards; the whole display framed by enough guitars, violins, clarinets and saxophones, all hung like sides of meat, to satisfy an entire band.

Until today Ginger had been saving for a mountain bike. All the lads, including his best mate Clyde, had bikes and it would make his paper round so much easier, but now, suddenly, saving up for the bike was forgotten.

Out of the whole shop, Ginger only had eyes for one thing. Half-hidden behind a pair of climbing boots lay a cassette recorder. As Ginger gazed longingly at it he unconsciously fingered the coins in his pocket, a whole week's pay his father had given him for doing the paper round.

The machine wasn't nearly as impressive as his big sister's ghetto-blaster, but Janice never let him anywhere near that. The one Ginger was drooling over was about the size of a packet of breakfast cereal. Mostly dull grey metal, it did have a sort of glass-fronted display panel on the front and although Ginger had no idea what it was for, he thought that made the machine look rather different and a bit special.

Ginger jumped as the fluorescent lights flickered into life and Mr Cumpsty appeared behind the door. An old man with white, tufty hair surrounding his bald patch, the thin, gold frames of his spectacles were held together with grey lumps of sticking plaster and his clothes were leftovers, ignored by customers with any shred of self-respect.

He turned over the sign to 'Open For Bargains' and drew back the rusty bolts. 'Oh, it's you again,' he murmured, gloomily wiping his long nose on a duster.

Hardly a day went by without Ginger popping in to check the price of something or other and he annoyed Mr Cumpsty by spending hours picking over the goods while he thought about it, or looked for a better bargain.

'So, what is it today?' Mr Cumpsty sighed. 'And keep your hands to yourself if you're not buying! It took me two hours to get that alarm clock you were fiddling with on Friday back together!'

'I'd have thought you'd be pleased to have a customer,' Ginger said. 'Especially at eight in the morning.'

'A customer, yes,' Mr Cumpsty said heavily, 'but you're what's known as "a mixed blessing"! You usually cost me more than you spend.'

'I'll be very careful, honest.'

'Mmm! Like the time you reduced a set of six Waterford crystal glasses to five? What is it you're *thinking* about today?'

'The cassette recorder in the middle of the window, next to the climbing boots.'

'Oh, that!' Mr Cumpsty's enthusiasm at the remotest possibility of a sale vanished.

'How much is it?'

'That's not really for sale.'

Ginger was amazed. They were words he'd never heard Mr Cumpsty use before. The old man was well known for being willing to steam his wallpaper off if anybody offered to buy it.

'Why not?' Ginger asked.

'Well,' Mr Cumpsty said uneasily, 'there's something wrong with it. I don't think it works properly.'

Another previously unheard confession! Only the things people wanted to sell *to* Mr Cumpsty were faulty; *his* stock was perfect in every detail until, that is, it got outside the shop. After which, to all complaints Mr Cumpsty would reply with a shrug, 'That's your bad luck! You should examine the goods *before* you buy them.' Though when you tried to follow his advice he got very angry and said, 'You can pull it apart *after* you've paid for it!'

'But what's wrong with the cassette recorder?' Ginger insisted.

'Look,' Mr Cumpsty said impatiently, 'I just don't want any more trouble.'

'Trouble?'

The old man's eyes darted about furtively. 'I've sold that blessed thing twice already and both times the customers brought it back and demanded their money back. The last one turned quite unpleasant.' Mr Cumpsty leaned forward and whispered confidentially, surrounding Ginger in a cloud of stale tobacco, 'Threatened me with the Trading Standards Officer!' Mr Cumpsty shuddered and picking up a cracked mug, he rinsed the foul words from his mouth with a swig of cold, weak tea.

'But what's the matter with it?' Ginger persisted.

Mr Cumpsty shrugged his thin shoulders. 'Search me. Perfectly all right one minute and the next you can't get a sound out of it. Almost as if it had a mind of its own,' he added darkly.

'Can I try it?' Ginger said eagerly.

'I've got far better ones that that.'

'And dearer, I bet!'

'Maybe a little more,' Mr Cumpsty admitted, 'but what I always say is, you gets what you pay for. Now this one's fifteen pounds . . .'

'But I haven't got fifteen pounds.'

'No, I suppose not,' Mr Cumpsty said wistfully, as if his sole ambition in life was to meet somebody who had.

'I'll give you a pound for the broken one,' Ginger offered brightly.

‘A POUND?’ Mr Cumpsty’s eyebrows shot up his face in alarm. ‘It cost me more than that.’

‘But you said it was no good, you didn’t want to sell it, so you’d only end up chucking it away. This way at least you’ll get a pound. I’ll take it off your hands and you won’t even have to bother to take it out to the dustbin.’

Mr Cumpsty thoughtfully rubbed his stubbly cheek. Reluctantly, he had to admit that the boy was right, a pound was better than nothing. ‘On two conditions,’ he added sharply.

‘Anything,’ Ginger rashly agreed.

‘One: you never bring the wretched thing back and two: you don’t tell anyone you bought it from me.’

‘Agreed.’

Ginger dropped the pound coin on to the counter and shot over to the window to grab his machine.

‘No, wait! I’ll get it out!’ Mr Cumpsty shrieked.

But it was too late.

As Ginger lifted up the machine his elbow dislodged a neatly stacked china teaset. For a split second it teetered uncertainly before falling forwards with a startling crash, shattering into fragments all over the window display.

Mr Cumpsty wailed, Ginger jumped back in horror and bumped into a ironing board which slid slowly sideways, triggering an avalanche. First it knocked over a display of cutlery canteens, which in turn collapsed on to a table full of LPs and sent them, sliding out of their covers, all over the floor.

Mr Cumpsty, seeing his shop being demolished, leapt forward. As he passed it, his bony shoulder nudged a set of shelves, rattling a row of plates displayed upright on their sides and making a large earthenware bust of Shakespeare on the very top shelf sway uncertainly.

Unfortunately Mr Cumpsty's carpet-slippered foot landed on one of the shiny records, slipped and sent him crashing to the floor. The vibration caused Shakespeare to rock all the more.

'Out!' Mr Cumpsty screamed, struggling to his feet.

'Let me help you up,' Ginger offered.

'*Out!*' he screamed again.

'I could help clear up.'

'OUT!'

Ginger, clutching his bargain, fled from the shop and slammed the door.

Shakespeare could stand no more. He fell from the shelf, hit Mr Cumpsty's bald head a glancing blow and smashed to pieces on the floor amongst the rest of the debris.

2

Signs of life

'Where've you been 'til now?' Dad asked, as Ginger shot round the end of the counter of his father's shop. 'You'll be late for school.'

'Plenty of time,' Ginger called back over his shoulder, as he cannoned through the shop and into the hall.

Mum poked her head round the kitchen door releasing the mouthwatering smell of sizzling bacon. 'Bacon butties for breakfast.'

Normally the smell alone would have been enough to cause Ginger to drown in his own saliva, but not today. He was already upstairs by his bedroom door. 'I'll be down in a minute, Mum.'

But Ginger was the Nutt family's human dustbin! He'd never been known to refuse food of any kind, with the sensible exceptions of cooked tomatoes and kidney beans. Shell-shocked, Mum wandered back towards the kitchen. Was Ginger trying to establish an illness alibi to avoid going to school?

Ginger, squatting in the middle of his unmade bed, prised the machine's back off and slotted the batteries into place. To his delight, yellow and green lights lit up in the front display panel!

Now all he needed to try it out was a cassette, but buying the batteries had left him skint. All the way home Ginger had been trying to work out how he could get his hands on one of his sister's cassettes without her knowing.

The solution came in a flash! Although he'd been up since seven o'clock doing his paper round, Janice, who was in the sixth form, didn't always have classes first thing. She was probably still enjoying what she called 'her beauty sleep'; not that Ginger had ever noticed any sign of improvement, no matter how late she slept.

He bounced downstairs two at a time. In the hall, lying against the wall under the coat hooks, was Janice's red tote bag which Ginger rudely called her kit of spare parts.

He feverishly scrabbled about inside. Normally the smell of make-up, old tights and school books would have been enough to put him off, but today it would have taken two pounds of festering liver and a live Rottweiller to keep him out.

Even so, he couldn't bring himself to *look* at the yucky contents, not after he found a pair of mud-stained P.E. knickers! He just felt about very warily with one hand, holding his nose with the other to avoid throwing up on the hall carpet.

'Geronimo!' he shouted as his fingers closed triumphantly round the unmistakable shiny plastic covers of two cassettes.

'What, love?' his mother called from the kitchen.

'A domino,' Ginger explained as he bounded hastily back up the stairs. 'There was one missing from the set and I've just found it.'

'Perhaps he really is ill,' Mum murmured, shaking her head.

Back in his room, Ginger shut the door and slipped the first cassette into the machine. It was Bananarama, but he felt beggars couldn't be choosers!

Excitedly Ginger pressed the Play button.

Nothing!

The cassette was going round, but no sound came out of the speaker, even though the volume was wound up to maximum. The yellow and green lights of the display panel hadn't budged.

Furious at wasting his money, Ginger wished he'd listened to Mr Cumpsty's warning after all. He pressed all the other switches one by one but although the tape spun back and forth on Fast Forward and Rewind, the machine remained totally silent.

'Ginger, I'm off to work,' Mum shouted up the stairs. 'If you don't come for your breakfast now you're going to be late!'

Angrily, though knowing it was useless, Ginger pushed every possible combination of switches before finally tossing the machine on to the bed.

Ginger was about to go and eat when he heard what sounded like the yawn of somebody waking from a particularly long and satisfying sleep.

Although Ginger could have sworn the noise came from his own room, he assumed he was mistaken. It must have been Janice waking; coming up for air, like a hippo rising from a pool.

But Janice was emerging from the bathroom, her head swathed in a towel and her face covered with a white face pack like a death mask.

'What are you doing?' she asked. To avoid cracking her drying face she spoke almost without moving her lips, like a bad ventriloquist.

'Nothing!' Ginger said, trying hard not to laugh.

'Then why are you skulking about on the landing. Have you been in my room?' Janice demanded.

'Janice, you've never looked better!'

Forgetting the pack, Janice snarled, 'Oh, you!'

A network of fine cracks instantly ran across her face until she resembled a pale imitation of Spiderman. 'Now I'll have to wash it off and start all over again!' she wailed, slamming back into the bathroom.

Ginger was in the kitchen eating his second succulent bacon butty when it suddenly turned to cardboard as an awful thought crossed his mind. Suppose, by fiddling about with the buttons on his machine he'd accidentally wiped Janice's tape?

She'd kill him, or worse still, let him live the rest of his life under constant torture!

Ginger dropped the half-eaten butty and for the hundredth time that morning pounded back up the stairs, snatched the tape out of the machine and thrust it back into the plastic case.

He was about to return it, when he realised the other tape he'd nicked was a blank. Even if his machine wouldn't play back, maybe it would record.

Ginger slipped the new tape into the machine and turned it so that the tiny grill marked Microphone faced him. He pressed the Record and Start buttons down firmly together. 'And if this doesn't work, I'll throw the thing out through the window.'

Ginger was thrilled to see the green and yellow LCD

lights rising and falling as he spoke. But he almost fell off the bed when they continued to move as the machine replied, 'I wouldn't do that if I were you!'

3

Sounds familiar?

'You can talk!' Ginger exclaimed, picking himself up off the carpet.

'There's nothing particularly clever about that. Even you can do that,' the machine said in a deep, slightly pompous and mechanical voice. 'My real claim to fame is my ability to think.'

'Machines can't think!' Ginger said scornfully. When the machine didn't reply he said it again.

'I heard you perfectly clearly the first time. But I decided *not* to answer,' he said snootily. 'Now, can I think or not?'

'That's not thinking. Thinking is working out problems, making decisions.'

'I see and you think I can't work things out for myself? Permit me to demonstrate!' There was a brief pause and suddenly Ginger's voice came out of the speaker. 'I won't throw the thing out through the window if this doesn't work.'

Ginger's mouth dropped open. 'That's my voice, but it's not what I said!'

'Exactly!' the machine said smugly. 'I thought about it, decided what you should have said and changed your words.'

'How?'

'Oh, that's comparatively simple stuff for me,' the machine boasted.

'But how?' Ginger insisted.

A sharp knock at the door and Janice's voice interrupted them. 'Ginger, who are you talking to?'

'Nobody,' then he added quickly, 'just myself!'

'You've got somebody in there with you.'

'No, I just told you.'

'You know you're not supposed to have anybody in the house while Mum's out.' Janice's voice rose above the threshold of pain as she continued to holler through the door. 'She's told you that a hundred times.'

Ginger pretended to own up. 'Okay! You're too smart for me.'

'I knew it!'

'Yes,' Ginger said, creeping up behind the door, 'I cannot tell a lie.'

'Who is it?' Janice demanded.

'Just me and Michael Jackson!' Ginger said, suddenly flinging his door open wide.

Janice, caught in her dressing gown and with a towel wound round her wet hair, leapt back with a startled scream while Ginger doubled up with laughter.

When she'd recovered Janice pushed past Ginger and scowled at the empty room. 'There's nobody here!'

'No,' Ginger said innocently. 'That's what I told you, but you wouldn't believe me.'

Janice still didn't believe her own eyes. 'There's nobody here.'

'You just said that. Michael rang at the last minute and said he couldn't make it after all.'

Janice still wasn't listening to him. 'But I distinctly heard voices.'

'Yes, I know.' Ginger nodded his head sympathetically. 'We did Joan of Arc in history, she kept hearing voices too and look how she ended up.'

Janice rounded on her brother. 'Listen, you,' she wagged a fat finger at him, 'if I hear one more sound coming from your room I'm telling Mum. It's time you were at school.' And she stalked off back to her room.

Ginger quietly closed his door and crept back to the bed. 'Sorry about that,' he apologised to the machine.

'Who on earth was that?'

'My sister Janice. Doesn't she look awful?'

'Excuse me! I'm a sound recorder, not a video camera! I can hear, but I can't see!'

'Sorry. Well, take my word for it.'

'She's certainly got a loud, unpleasant voice,' the machine complained. 'It's quite strained my compressors!'

'Keep your voice down!' Ginger hissed.

'You turned my volume control up,' the machine pointed out. 'I may be very advanced, but I can't do everything for myself.'

'Oh, right!' Ginger wound down the volume a little. 'How's that?'

'Testing, testing! One, two, three,' the machine said in a very bored voice. 'Is that better?'

'Yes. Now, where were we? You were just telling me something when she knocked . . .'

'Oh,' the machine interrupted, 'you want replay.'

Before Ginger could answer the machine repeated their earlier conversation. 'Oh, that's comparatively simple stuff for me,' from the machine was followed by a voice which Ginger thought wasn't like his saying, 'But how?' Then, after the knock on the door, came Janice screeching like a nail being drawn across glass, 'Ginger, who are you talking to?'

Ginger was astonished. 'Wow! That's incredible!'

'Oh, it's nothing really, but what you really wanted to know was how could I change your words. Besides a memory chip, which stores my voice and some other giszmos, I've also got a built-in sampler. The kind you get in some superior electronic keyboards. I can store your voice in my memory bank and apply it to my vast dictionary of words. After that I can either replay your words, like any common cassette recorder, or make you say something completely different.'

'I've never heard of a machine that could do that before.'

'There isn't one.' The machine's pride was tinged with sadness. 'I am a prototype. My inventor, a brilliant man called Carter-Symes, went bankrupt before he could market the idea. Lots of people were dying to get their hands on me but, because he couldn't pay off his debts, his house was cleared in his absence by the bailiffs. Which is how I ended up in the shop of that dreadful man.'

'Mr Cumpsty?'

'Yes,' the machine said gloomily. 'Oh, the shame of it! A scientific breakthrough like me, state-of-the-art technology, ending up in a scruffy second-hand shop!'

'Three times,' Ginger pointed out. 'Two people

bought you and took you back because you didn't work.'

'*Wouldn't* work!' the machine corrected. 'Not for them!'

'Yes and you did the same thing to me, which nearly got you chucked in the bin!'

'Yes, well, I was unhappy. Do you know, they wanted me to play something called Heavy Metal? It would probably have blown my extremely sensitive speaker.'

'I only wanted you to play Bananarama,' Ginger pointed out.

'Doesn't anybody want to listen to Beethoven or Mozart any more?' the machine sighed.

'I don't,' Ginger said, pulling a face, 'and you won't be much use if you won't play the music I want to hear.'

The machine considered the point and reluctantly agreed. 'But there are other reasons for keeping me. I have a number of advanced facilities you have yet to explore. For instance, my memory bank is crammed with a wide range of sound effects.'

Before Ginger could ask what possible use they could be, the machine proceeded to demonstrate by repeating, in the original version, what Ginger had said earlier. 'If this doesn't work I'll throw the thing out through the window.'

But this time the machine added a loud and convincing smash of glass!

Ginger laughed, but the laughter died as Janice burst into the room, her hair hanging down in wet rat's tails. 'What have you done now?' she demanded.

Then she stopped dead, staring at the window she'd just heard break, but which was clearly still in one piece.

'I could have sworn I heard . . .' but Janice's voice trailed off.

'What did you think you heard *this* time?' Ginger asked innocently whilst trying hard not to laugh and hoping the machine wouldn't give him away.

'I had the hair dryer on,' she said, 'but I could have sworn I heard voices again and the sound of breaking glass.'

'Maybe it was somebody throwing a stone at one of the empty houses,' Ginger suggested, stifling a delighted giggle.

Janice rushed over to the window but there was nobody in sight. She rounded on Ginger and her eyes narrowed with suspicion. 'You're up to something, I know you are and I'll fix you good and proper tonight when Mum gets back!'

This time, when she left, she slammed every door she passed through so hard that the entire house shook.

'Come on,' Ginger said, picking up the machine, 'I'd better not be late for school, I'll be in enough trouble when Janice snitches to Mum!'

'Why are you worried about any lie your sister might tell when I can always play back exactly what she said.'

'Of course!' Ginger couldn't believe his luck. At last, an ally in the continuing battle against his sister! Then a thought struck him. 'I think I'd like to save that for later. By the way, what do I call you?'

'Call me?' The machine sounded baffled.

'I mean, I'm Ginger but what's your name?'

'I'm the Carter-Symes 2000,' it said proudly.

'That's a description not a name! I'll call you Cass!'

'Cass?' the machine hissed back with distaste.

'Yes, Cass the cassette recorder, get it?'

'How very witty!' the machine groaned.

As they were about to walk out on to the landing, Cass hissed, 'Don't forget to switch me off. Apart from the fact that it gives me a little rest, then you won't waste my batteries. I am rather powerful and you only bought ordinary batteries, which won't last very long.'

'I'm sorry, they were all I could afford.'

'Yes, well, next time remember, I prefer long life batteries.'

'Yes, I will,' Ginger promised.

'And if they could be "green" batteries,' Cass continued, 'Carter-Symes was always very environmentally-conscious . . .'

'Yes, all right!' Ginger said, firmly pressing the off switch. There was a slight yawn, followed by silence. 'I think I'm going to enjoy this!' Ginger said to himself, slipping Cass into his school bag.

4

Saved by the bell

'Hi, Ginger! Where've you been? The first bell's gone.'

Clyde, his best mate, greeted him with that grin of his that never went away. He was leaning against the school gate. For years they'd lived in the same street, until Ginger's Mum and Dad had scraped up the money to buy the newsagent's shop. Now, even though they were on the opposite sides of town they still spent most of their spare time together.

All the way to school, Ginger had been wondering whether to share his amazing new buy with Clyde. Usually they never kept secrets from each other, but this time Ginger reckoned he could have a bit of fun with Cass and Clyde before letting him in on the machine's astonishing powers.

It wasn't until first break, while they were sharing a bag of crisps, that Ginger slipped a hand inside his school bag, switched Cass to Record and eased the bag round until it was close to Clyde. 'So, what are you doing Saturday?' Ginger asked innocently.

'Dunno. Dad says I've got to cut the grass before we disappear into a jungle, that's about all.'

Ginger, his hand still inside his bag, pushed the

Rewind button and then replayed Clyde's words.

'Hey! What you got there?' Clyde said, diving for the bag. Before Ginger could stop him, Clyde had pulled the machine out and was admiring it. 'That's brill!'

But no sooner was it out, than a meaty hand reached between them and a hoarse voice demanded, 'Give us that 'ere!'

Ginger hastily snatched Cass back from Clyde and they both jumped back as Crusher Williams, a fifth form bully, made another, more determined grab for the machine.

A crowd from Ginger's class watched with interest, relieved that they weren't Crusher's target. He was well known for helping himself to anything he wanted and had several times been up before the head for running a protection racket. He took younger kids' dinner money, using blatant threats of what would happen to them to demonstrate why they needed protection.

Crusher's reputation as a hard man went back to when he was still in the second year and he'd broken a sixth former's arm. He no longer needed to actually use violence, the threat alone was enough.

'I said, give us that 'ere!' Crusher repeated menacingly.

Ginger felt his stomach tighten into knots. 'What do you want?' he said, trying to bluff his way out. Although he was scared, Ginger was determined not to give Cass up without a struggle. His only real hope was to play for time, on the off chance that a teacher on playground duty would notice what Crusher was up to.

'Leave him alone, Crusher!' Clyde said, sticking up for his mate.

'I'll wipe that stupid smile off your face for you, Clyde Bowen, if you don't mind your own business,' Crusher said, thrusting up a bunched fist, millimetres from Clyde's nose.

The distraction gave Ginger enough time to dodge behind a group of bigger lads, but they offered little protection and Crusher shouldered them roughly aside like a Chieftain tank. 'I told you, Nutt,' he snarled, holding out his hand for the cassette recorder, 'to 'and that over.'

'It's mine!' Ginger tried to sound brave, but his courage was fading, there was still no sign of a teacher and he was cornered, his back pressed against the wooden planks of the bike shed with Crusher blocking any possible escape.

'I'll count up to three and then . . . !' Crusher, with his back to the crowd, shut his mouth tightly and punched one beefy fist into the palm of his other hand. But then, though Ginger could see his lips were tightly closed, as far as the other kids were concerned, his voice went on, 'And then I'll apologise for being such a slob.'

During the stunned silence which descended on the playground, Crusher's mouth dropped open.

Ginger suddenly realised he'd forgotten to switch Cass off.

'What did you just say, Crusher?' a boy called out from the audience.

Crusher took a deep breath to speak, but Cass got in first. 'What's the matter? Have you got cloth ears or somethin'? I said I'd apologise for being such a slob.'

Everyone burst into hysterical laughter. Crusher's face went red with fury as he whirled round to face them and roared, 'Who do you think you're laughing at?'

But, even though they kept well away from his tightly bunched fists, they laughed even louder.

'Why don't you kiss and make up?' another boy suggested.

Crusher lunged at him, missed, and staggered off, dazed and bewildered, as the bell sounded for the end of break.

'How on earth did you get Crusher to back off like that?' Clyde asked.

'He didn't . . . I mean, I didn't . . .' Ginger looked around. 'It's a bit difficult to explain here, Clyde. I'll tell you later.'

'Quiet!' Mr Lodge yelled at the top of his voice as he swept along the corridor and unlocked the door. They groaned. Even in a good mood Mr Lodge needed treating with care; Mr Lodge in a bad mood was like being within range of an unguided nuclear missile. Hardly anybody in the class escaped the rough edge of Mr Lodge's tongue as he strode between the desks spitting out facts about the English Civil War with all the rapidity and friendliness of a Kalashnikov.

He also indulged his quirk of addressing the class from behind them, shouting at anybody who dared turn round, 'Face the front, boy!' When he tired of that, Mr Lodge crept silently up each aisle and, striking at random, suddenly brought his ruler down on the desk of his innocent victim with a loud crack.

When they jumped he screeched, 'Sit still, don't wriggle!'

Unless you were actually writing in his lessons it was wise to keep both hands off the desk because he didn't mind 'accidentally' swiping knuckles in the process.

Towards the end of the lesson he asked them to take out their homework and leave it, open, on their desks.

As Ginger bent down to get his history exercise book from his bag, Clyde, at the next desk, looked across and said in an agonized whisper, 'I'm dead! I forgot to do it!'

'Silence!' Mr Lodge roared. He marched round the desks, collecting up the work, making sarcastic comments like, 'Five lines and three blots don't make a satisfactory essay'.

He deliberately left Clyde until the very last and when he was towering over him, with icy politeness, he asked, 'Been using invisible ink, Bowen?'

Clyde knew there was nothing he could say that would get him out of trouble.

Ginger chipped in helpfully, 'We did it together at my house and he left his there, sir.'

'Shut up,' Mr Lodge snapped, without bothering to turn round, 'unless you want to be a cracked Nutt!'

The class giggled dutifully at this old joke. Mr Lodge silenced them with a glare and turned back to Clyde. 'I asked you a question, Bowen, and wipe that impertinent grin off your face!'

Ginger felt so sorry for Clyde who couldn't help his grin. It was mostly nerves, but it always annoyed teachers, particularly ones like Mr Lodge.

'I'm still waiting, Bowen!'

Clyde wriggled uncomfortably. 'I forgot it.'

'Sir!' snapped Mr Lodge.

'. . . Sir.'

'Do you mean,' Mr Lodge persisted, 'you forgot it, as in Nutt's threadbare excuse, or you forgot to do it all?'

Fear widened Clyde's grin further. 'Forgot to do it, Sir!'

The silence which followed seemed to last for ever. 'So,' Mr Lodge said eventually. 'Not only did you not bother to do the work I set you, but Nutt agreed to lie to protect you!'

Mr Lodge stood poised for the kill, detentions would soon be thrown around like confetti when a brilliant idea flashed across Ginger's mind. He bent down, hissed something to Cass and then sat up, fiddling with his watch.

Ginger was barely upright before a loud bell suddenly rang out and everybody started noisily gathering their stuff together.

'Sit still!' the teacher shouted. 'It's not the end of the period yet!'

'Yes, it is, sir,' the class chorused, glad of any excuse. 'The bell's gone.'

Angry, but puzzled, Mr Lodge, who prided himself on accuracy, held up his watch. 'But it's only twelve minutes past.'

'You must have forgotten to wind it, sir,' Ginger suggested politely, showing Mr Lodge his own recently adjusted watch which said quarter past.

'Good heavens, so it is.' Mr Lodge, who had another class to go to, looked flustered. 'Right, you'd better get off,' he spluttered, the subject of Clyde's homework completely forgotten in the confusion.

5

Funny business

'Hey,' Clyde said, 'have you heard? Crusher's gone home sick!'

'He's been sick all his life!' Ginger replied with a grin.

'You promised you'd explain all that business with Crusher,' Clyde insisted.

Wandering round the playground, burping many happy returns of the school dinner hamburger, seemed the ideal opportunity.

'Well, you heard what happened,' Ginger began. 'Crusher apologised, but he didn't *really* speak at all.'

'Why, have you learned to be a ventriloquist?'

'I don't need to,' Ginger said proudly, pulling the tape machine out of his bag. 'I've got Cass to do it for me.'

Clyde looked baffled. 'Who's Cass?'

'This is Cass, the fantastic tape recorder I bought at Mr Cumpsty's.'

'Oh yes?' Clyde said in disbelief. He was so used to the 'bargains' Ginger picked up from that dump that he couldn't believe this one would be any better.

'But he isn't just a recorder. He's only got to hear somebody's voice to say something else exactly like them.'

‘Oh yes?’ Clyde repeated. Why was Ginger referring to the tape recorder as ‘he’?

‘And that’s not all. You know the bell went off early in History?’

‘Yes, saved my bacon, that did.’

‘That was Cass too,’ Ginger said proudly.

This seemed more believable to Clyde. ‘You mean you recorded the bell before class and then played it back when things were getting sticky?’

‘No! I asked Cass to use his sound effects bank.’

Clyde was really worried now!

‘But, Clyde, you mustn’t tell anybody.’

‘Don’t worry,’ Clyde said. ‘I wouldn’t have the guts to tell anybody a story like that!’

‘Don’t you believe me?’

‘Do I look as if I eat nails?’ Clyde demanded.

‘All right, I’ll show you!’ Ginger pressed Record and held the machine up to Clyde’s mouth. ‘Say something to him.’

‘I think you’re a few sandwiches short of a picnic!’

‘Right.’ Ginger stopped recording, too busy demonstrating Cass’s powers to realise that Clyde was speaking his mind. ‘Now, Cass,’ Ginger whispered to the machine, ‘do your stuff! Make him say something else!’

Silence.

‘Cass, come on, show Clyde what you can do!’

‘Maybe you pressed the wrong button,’ Clyde suggested helpfully.

‘I don’t have to press any buttons, he can do it all on his own once he’s heard somebody. Like he did with Crusher.’

But when Ginger pressed Rewind, followed by Playback, all that came out was Clyde repeating, 'I think you're a few sandwiches short of a picnic!' to which Clyde finally added, 'Ain't that the truth!' And when Ginger tried to make excuses, Clyde scoffed, 'Maybe he's tired!'

'You could be right,' Ginger agreed.

Clyde's eyebrows shot up. 'I don't believe this!'

'I mean his batteries could be running low.'

Clyde began to edge away. 'I'm off to play footie with Ali, are you coming, or what?'

Ginger pressed the Battery Check switch and although the needle didn't move to the top of the scale, there was still plenty of power left. 'The batteries seem okay. I don't understand what's the matter.'

'I'll see you later then,' Clyde said and ran off to join Ali and the others.

Ginger stood, alone, shaking the machine, angry with Cass for not working and equally cross that Clyde refused to believe his explanation. 'I knew I should have thrown you away! Waste of money you were.'

Ginger nearly dropped Cass when he said, 'I thought we had been through all that before?'

'Why wouldn't you speak while Clyde was here?'

'I'm not a sideshow at a fairground,' Cass protested indignantly. 'I'm a scientific instrument. I may be down on my luck at the moment, but I still have some pride.'

'Made me look a right idiot!' Ginger grumbled.

'I don't think that's very fair. Only this morning you said you wanted to keep me a secret but I saved you from that horrible boy and I didn't hesitate to ring the bell when you asked me.'

'Yes, I know, but I wanted to show you off to Clyde.'

'But the more people know what I can really do, the more likely somebody is to steal me.'

'I hadn't thought of that.'

'No, but I had. Carter-Symes, my inventor, knew I was in danger of being stolen from the first moment. He believed the fewer people knew I existed the better. One manufacturer was particularly anxious to get his hands on me and didn't mind how he did it.'

'Why didn't he buy you?'

'He refused to pay a penny until he had examined my interior. Insisted I was all trickery and wouldn't believe otherwise until he'd taken me apart. Ugh,' Cass would have shuddered if he could, 'the thought of people prying around my insides with their nasty little screwdrivers makes my transistors feel quite weak.'

'But you can understand what they meant,' Ginger said. 'Clyde didn't believe a word I said about you and he's my friend. So why should they?'

'It was merely an excuse so that he could steal Carter-Symes' idea. Once he'd found out how I worked he would never have paid up. I wouldn't be surprised if he's still searching for me.'

'Well, in that case, you're safer with me, aren't you?'

'I wouldn't be too sure. He's a desperate, greedy man who'll stop at nothing to get his hands on me. On three separate occasions, people broke into Carter-Symes' house. That's why I was so reluctant, just now, to do what you asked.'

'But Clyde's safe, he's my best mate.'

'Very well, if you say so. I quite understand you wanting to boast about me to your friends,' Cass said proudly, 'but it would only take one slip for the secret to be out and before long everybody would know.'

'Clyde can keep his mouth shut when he wants to.'

'But this is such a public place for a full-scale demonstration. Anybody could have overheard. Perhaps next time, you could choose a more private location?'

'Yes, I see what you mean. Anyway, you've got his voice recorded in your memory, haven't you?'

'Yes.'

'Great!'

But for the rest of break Ginger was forced to watch Clyde and Ali playing footie and Clyde, though he did give Ginger some very odd, pitying looks, didn't say much for the rest of the day.

They were about to set off home when Ginger asked Clyde if he was going to come and help deliver the papers.

'Not tonight. I'm a bit busy,' Clyde muttered uncomfortably.

'Oh, yes? Doing what?' It was Ginger's turn not to believe a word.

Clyde shrugged. 'Things.'

'Oh, well, if that's the way you feel about it,' Ginger said and walked home in a huff.

6

Family business

Gloomily, Ginger plodded through the dark on his paper round, too preoccupied with his thoughts to notice he was being followed by a man in steel-rimmed glasses, his raincoat collar turned up, who hugged the shadows.

Usually Ginger spent his paper round doing silly things. Like the tug-of-war through the letter box with the dog at 23 Mafeking Street, which ended with the dog shredding the newspaper. Or there was balancing the folded newspaper halfway through a letter box, hitting the end hard with the palm of his hand. The effect of this was similar to the hammer of a gun striking a bullet and sent the newspaper shooting out like a heat-seeking ballistic missile!

But that night, Ginger was too fed up about breaking friends with Clyde to bother.

Eventually he delivered his last paper, carelessly pushing it right through the brass letter box, forgetting its heavily sprung flap which snapped down across his knuckles like a rat trap.

'What an *amazing* day this has turned into!' he muttered, nursing his grievances – and his pinched fingers – as he trudged home.

Being a corner shop, there were three doors. One opened into the shop, one was a back door from the kitchen into a small yard and the third was a side door which opened from Adventure Street straight into the hallway and stairs of the house.

The man who'd followed Ginger watched him go in through the shop doorway and then melted into the darkness, heading for the town centre.

Ginger's dad was hunched over the counter doing sums on the back of an old envelope.

Ginger knew Dad was adding up how much money he'd taken in the shop that day to see if he'd made any profit. He went through this performance every night and the answer rarely improved his temper.

When they'd first found the shop, Mum and Dad had described it as 'a Golden Opportunity', just like the gaudy posters that appeared at sales time in chain store windows.

The Nutts had put all their savings, every bit they'd managed to scrape together over the years, into buying the business and taking over the lease of the property.

Although Ginger hadn't been very keen on moving away from Clyde and the area he'd grown up in, when he realised that he'd be able to read, for free, every comic that came out, he'd decided it could have its advantages.

He dreamt of lying in bed reading comics while slowly chomping through the shop's entire stock of chocolate bars, fizz bombs, Everton toffee and endless varieties of bubble gum. He reckoned it was going to be like locking up a pig in a pastry shop!

Dad quickly corrected him. Whilst Ginger could

borrow comics, he was never allowed to keep any and the only sweets Ginger ate had to be paid for out of his own money, which must be earned by taking paper rounds night and morning.

Even so, at first everything was fine, but then, very quickly, houses in Adventure Street were boarded up, as people moved out and nobody moved in. Then the same started happening to the houses round the corner in Khartoum Street.

Soon, from living in the middle of a busy community, where everybody popped into the shop all day long the Nutts found themselves almost isolated. Eventually so little money was coming in that Mum had to go back to her old typing job.

At first Dad thought the council was buying up the properties, but after a visit to the town hall he discovered that they had been bought by a property company. They had put in a huge planning application to knock down all houses between Adventure Street and Khartoum Street, where Ginger's gran once lived, and replace it with a hypermarket. 'I expect you'll be next,' the man at the town hall had said. 'Yours is the only property they don't own.'

When Dad told Mum she sighed, 'We'll just have to sell then, won't we?'

'But we don't own the property,' Dad pointed out. 'We only bought the business and all we've got besides is the remains of a lease which runs out in five years' time.'

Mum began to look worried. 'So our landlords could sell the building without even asking us?'

Dad nodded.

Sure enough, a week later a letter came from the property company, which announced they were the new lease owners and they would like to buy back the remaining portion of the lease.

'Which means we'll have to move out straight away,' Dad explained to the family.

'They can't *make* us do that, can they?' Ginger asked.

'No, they can't.'

'But I think we ought to accept their offer,' Mum said.

'So do I,' murmured Janice. 'It's getting really spooky living round here with all the boarded-up houses, especially at night.'

'Frightened the ghosties might get you?' Ginger teased.

Janice aimed a blow at Ginger's bright red head.

'It's all very well to joke about it,' Mum said, 'but you never know who you'll meet coming out of those empty houses. There's a tramp sleeping in the outside lavatory of number fifteen and remember those squatters who broke into one of the houses and started a fire? I think Janice is right, we should sell.'

'But have you seen how much they're offering?' Dad passed the letter over to Mum. 'It's not a fraction of what we paid because it only covers the remainder of the lease. When we moved in, not only did we have to buy the old stock but most of our money went on buying the goodwill of the business . . .'

'What's "goodwill"?' Ginger chipped in.

'You might well ask!' Dad said bitterly. 'It's a big sum of money you hand over to the previous owners for the business they've built up over the years. The people who sold it to us obviously knew what was going to happen, because when we bought it there were hundreds of customers and now most of them have gone. So now there's no goodwill for the company to buy. They just want us out of the building so they're only offering chicken feed. Which means all our savings disappear down the drain!'

'Unless we stay?' Mum asked.

Dad nodded. 'But to do that we'd have to build up the business again from scratch, replace all the customers we've lost.'

And that was what they'd tried to do over the last six months. Dad had gone round houses for miles around, knocking on doors and asking if they'd like papers delivered. Quite a few had placed orders but, because they weren't close to the shop, Ginger's delivery round became much longer and the new customers only dropped in once a month to pay their bills. So it wasn't surprising that Dad did his sums every night, or that the answer was never very good.

'How's it going, Dad?' Ginger asked as he stowed his delivery bag away under the counter.

'Well, it's no better, but it's no worse either.'

A high-pitched scream from Mum sent them running out to the kitchen. 'What's up, love?' Dad asked.

'I opened the back door and there was this great horrible rat, just sitting there grinning at me!'

Dad shook his head. 'I've put poison down, but as more people move out, I'm afraid there'll be more rats. They've eaten up all the scraps folks left behind and so they're bound to come up here.'

'People dumping their rubbish doesn't help,' said Janice.

'That's right!' Mum agreed.

Dad nodded. 'I expect it won't be long before one of those sacks comes sailing over our wall!'

'I'd chuck it back at them!' Ginger said fiercely.

'They won't do it where they see anybody around. But it wouldn't hurt to take car numbers if you do spot someone out there, then we can report them to the police.'

Suddenly the shop bell rang and they all froze in astonishment.

'A customer!' Dad said, perking up. 'Mustn't let them get away!'

While Dad bustled off into the shop Ginger asked, 'What's for tea, Mum?'

'Bubble and squeak.'

'Wicked!' Ginger said. 'I'm starving. Can I have a biscuit while I'm waiting?'

'It'll only be a couple of minutes,' Mum pointed out. 'I'll dish up as soon as your dad's served that customer and shut the shop.'

'I can't wait that long,' Ginger protested.

Mum was about to answer when Dad came back looking white-faced and angry. 'What on earth's the matter?'

'That wasn't a customer,' Dad said.

'Who was it then?'

'Two blokes. Said they worked for the property company. At least one of them did, the other guy hardly spoke, just stood there like a great gorilla.'

'What did they want?'

'They wanted us to reconsider our decision not to sell.'

'What did you say?'

'I told them to get . . . I said we wouldn't.'

'That's all right then.'

'Except then the gorilla said I might be sorry I hadn't changed my mind, because he knew ways of making people feel sorry they'd even been born!'

7

Raising the alarm

After tea, when Ginger went up to his room, he switched Cass on and there was a fairly loud yawn before Cass said, 'Yes, what can I do for you?'

'I just wanted somebody to talk to while I do my homework.'

'What is it tonight?' Cass asked, though he didn't sound particularly interested.

'Maths.'

'Ah!'

'I don't suppose you're any good at maths.'

'I fear not. Carter-Symes made me literate, but not numerate. He had plans for incorporating a talking calculator,' Cass sighed wistfully, 'but they never came to anything.'

'What do you think's happened to him?'

'Carter-Symes? I am positive he's searching for me. You have to remember that I represent the culmination of twelve years of his work. He'll be devastated about losing me.'

'I think we're going to lose the shop,' Ginger said and then had to explain to Cass everything that had happened, including tonight's threats.

Mum knocked and walked in with a tray. 'I've brought you some milk and biscuits,' she said. 'How's your homework going?'

'Nearly finished, Mum,' he lied.

She was about to leave when she asked, 'Were you talking to yourself just now?'

'Me?' Ginger opened his eyes wide. 'No, Mum.'

She shook her head. 'Really, I could have sworn I heard two voices.'

'Janice said the same thing this morning. Maybe somebody's broken into the house next door.'

'The voices sounded too close, as if they were coming from this room, but you may be right. I'll get your father to check before we come to bed. Don't stay up late. Good night.'

'Good night.'

His parents always went to bed early because the newspapers dropped on the doorstep at half-past five in the morning, for them to sort and mark with house numbers ready for delivery by seven.

Ginger was still struggling with his maths when he heard his father come up to bed and shortly afterwards his sister did her impression of a baby elephant in the room next to his.

It was gone ten when Ginger put Cass on his bedside table and climbed into bed.

'Good night, Cass.'

'Good night, Ginger.'

Ginger turned out his bedside light before he noticed the yellow and green glow of Cass's display. 'I'd better switch you off now, so's not to waste the batteries.'

'You can just press the Pause button and leave me on stand-by.'

'Stand-by?'

'Yes, I have a built-in real-time clock, you only have to tell me what time you want waking and I take care of the rest.'

Ginger was impressed. 'Gosh.'

'Oh, you haven't begun to explore half of my special facilities,' Cass boasted.

'It's ten past ten now. Could you wake me at ten to seven in time to do my paper round?'

'I presume you mean 0650 hours?'

'Yes.'

'That will be quite all right, although it is a little earlier than Carter-Symes ever rose,' Cass said wearily. Then he asked, cautiously, 'You don't snore, do you?'

Ginger laughed. 'I don't think so, I've never stayed awake long enough to find out! No, I'm sure I don't.'

'Thank goodness for that. Carter-Symes did. Listen.'

Ginger nearly jumped out of bed as Cass produced a noise similar to a hiccupping buzz-saw cutting through sheet metal.

Janice banged on the wall and Ginger banged back.

'That's an awful noise,' Ginger whispered to Cass.

'Kept me awake all night long!'

'Have you stored any other recordings of Carter-Symes?'

'I kept that one in my sound effects collection. I haven't got any of his actual speech. Though, of course, I have stored his speech pattern and I can apply that to my dictionary in the normal way.'

'Can I hear him?'

A young man's voice came out of the speaker. 'Without doubt the Carter-Symes 2000 is my most magnificent achievement to date, a real scientific breakthrough. I shall search tirelessly for him, even if I have to go to the ends of the earth.'

Ginger laughed until he realised what Cass had just said using Carter-Symes' voice. 'I suppose, if he found you, he'd want to take you away from me?'

'I certainly hope so,' Cass said.

'Oh,' Ginger said sadly.

'I don't mean he'd steal me. I'm sure he'd give you back whatever you paid.'

But as Ginger went to sleep, the room lit by the dim glow of Cass's display lights, he began to think that it was a good thing Cass had refused to work in the playground. Ginger made up his mind to do whatever was necessary to make sure that Cass would never be found. Even if that meant Clyde could never know about him!

Ginger woke with a terrible start to discover that not only was Cass's light on, but he was emitting the most horrible two-tone howl, loud enough to wake the whole house.

Ginger thought it must be time to get up, so he switched on his light and looked at his watch. It was only midnight! 'Cass! Have you gone mad?'

Cass stopped howling. 'I thought I'd never be able to wake you.'

'But it's midnight! I asked you to wake me at seven.'

'My smoke detector went off and I automatically

went into alarm mode. It's given me a dreadful headache!'

There was a thunderous knocking on Ginger's door and Dad shouted, 'Ginger! Janice! Get up! The house is on fire!' The door burst open and Dad, in his dressing gown with a damp handkerchief clutched over his mouth, appeared in a swirl of black smoke. 'The stairs are on fire, we'll have to climb out through our room at the back.' He disappeared into Janice's room.

'Don't forget me, will you?' Cass hissed.

'No fear!' Ginger said, grabbing Cass and an anorak.

Coughing his way through the thick smoke, Ginger ran with the others along the landing and into his parent's bedroom where they firmly closed the door. Their room overlooked the back yard, and just under the window was the roof of the small lean-to building Dad used as a stockroom.

'I'll go first,' Dad said, 'and find the stepladder for the rest of you.'

They watched Dad sliding down the tiled roof. Although they'd shut the bedroom door to keep the fire out, smoke was seeping in and there was already a terrific build-up of heat.

Janice glanced anxiously over her shoulder. 'Has Dad phoned the fire brigade?'

'Yes,' Mum said.

Dad shouted out from below, 'Ladder's ready, come on!'

Janice went first. Just as Ginger was going to climb out Mum noticed his cassette recorder. 'What a strange thing to remember to bring with you at a time like this!'

Ginger didn't reply, but scrambled out of the window. Frightened of slipping, he eased himself cautiously down the cold, damp tiles until his slippers felt the safety of the gutter. He was turning to look for the ladder when he heard a car start up on the waste ground behind the house. Peering into the darkness he could just make out the shape of a grey car, moving slowly over the bumpy ground towards the road.

Dad called out anxiously. 'This is no time to stop and admire the view, Ginger! Get your foot on here now.' His father guided Ginger by gripping his ankle until he was safely on the stepladder. The moment Ginger was down Dad called up to his wife to follow.

'Have you seen what Ginger's brought with him?' she said when they were all four safely in the yard. 'A tape recorder!'

'Well, I must admit I did grab yesterday's takings,' Dad laughed producing a thin roll of notes.

'And I bet Janice has brought her make-up bag! In case there are any good-looking firemen!' Ginger giggled and ducked to avoid her blow.

Fortunately, the fire was mainly confined to the hall and stairs at the side of the house and didn't affect the shop at all. The firemen soon had it under control with the minimum amount of mess.

'Good job you found it so early,' the Chief Fire Officer said, 'otherwise it could have been very nasty. You were lucky to have a makeshift fire-escape too.'

'I wouldn't have minded being rescued,' Janice said, fluttering her eyelashes at a blond fireman she thought looked like her favourite actor in one of the Australian

TV soaps. 'Could you show me how you do a fireman's lift?'

To her annoyance the fireman quickly walked away.

The Chief Officer said to Dad, as they were packing up, 'The Fire Investigation Officer will be round tomorrow.'

Dad looked surprised. 'Why?'

'Well, it's not for me to say, but when we broke the side door down we found the end of a bit of rag still hanging out of the letter box. Somebody must have pushed a petrol-soaked rag through and set fire to it!'

After the fire crew left and the family had been to inspect the damage to the smoke-blackened hall, they were sitting in the kitchen, trying to ignore the horrible smell, drinking hot chocolate, when Dad said, 'I bet you anything those two blokes who came into the shop this evening had something to do with this.'

Mum nodded. 'Maybe, but it could just as easily have been a tramp from one of the old houses.'

But Dad wasn't convinced. 'Why would they want to set fire to our house? No, I reckon it was those two, trying to scare us out.'

'Well, they nearly succeeded,' Mum admitted. 'You were fast asleep and if it hadn't been for the smoke alarm, I'd never have woken up until it was too late! We could all have been burnt alive in our beds.'

They all shuddered at the thought.

Then Dad slowly turned to Mum. 'You must have been dreaming, June, we haven't got a smoke alarm.'

Ginger kept his smile to himself.

8

Hatching a plot

It wasn't until the next morning before school, while Ginger was telling Clyde about the threats and the fire, that Ginger remembered the grey car. Ginger knew now how he could get his own back on Clyde for not believing that Cass could talk.

'This car was lurking about on the waste land,' Ginger explained, 'and I'm sure it had something to do with the fire. So I reckon it would be worth keeping a lookout to see if it comes back again and the best place to do that from is the tree house in the old churchyard.'

The original church had been destroyed by the Puritans and the next was bombed during the Second World War. Only the tower remained, the rest was reduced to a dangerous shell which had to be demolished.

Throughout the years, all sorts of other possible uses for the land had been suggested but nothing ever came of these plans and during the fifty years since the war the old churchyard had rapidly turned into an overgrown jungle of brambles, nettles and rose-bay willow herb.

Amongst these, flowering plants had sprung up from the garden rubbish people dumped there; snowdrops, daffodils, lupins, primroses and the orange trumpets of nasturtiums bloomed in season. There were rose bushes which had once been planted on the old graves, a thick copse made up of one family's discarded Christmas trees and an oak tree supposed to be well over three hundred years old.

Pigeons adopted the tower for nesting sites, stray cats stalked the long grass and kids built dens under the self-seeded bushes which had sprung up amongst the thick, head-high weeds.

During an expedition in the churchyard, Ginger had found the remains of a tree house lodged in the branches of a tall, bushy, evergreen fir. Its base was a solid wooden pallet of the kind lifted on to lorries by fork-lift trucks. The sides had been mainly built from bits of old packing cases and carried fading stencilled messages such as 'USE NO HOOKS' and 'JAFFA'. One piece that said 'THIS WAY UP' had been carefully nailed into place upside down.

By the time Ginger found the tree house, all the children who'd once lived in Adventure Street had moved out, so he'd adopted it as his own. It made a fantastic lookout point. He could see not only right up Adventure Street but also out across the waste ground behind the houses and right down to the canal tow-path that ran along the bottom end of the churchyard. Grown-ups rarely set foot in the churchyard, except for a few fishermen and others who used the well-trodden path to reach the canal.

Ginger thought it was a great place, if a bit spooky.

Not that there were any dead bodies buried there any more. Before the demolition work had begun, all the graves had been cleared but a few very old, lichen covered gravestones remained, set in concrete against the crumbling stone wall that enclosed the yard. Their gaunt outlines served as a ghostly reminder to Ginger and Clyde of what the place had once been.

The only other relic was a small white cherub carved in marble. It must have once been part of a memorial stone that had got overlooked during the clearance. Now it stood alone and though moss grew in the cherub's crevices, and it only had one-and-a-half wings left, it still smiled bravely, one of its chipped fingers eternally pointing upwards to Heaven.

Ginger had often kept watch from the tree house and he'd never seen anybody go near the cherub yet the weeds never smothered it. Not only that but every now and then, a small circlet of fresh flowers appeared on the cherub's tiny head.

The cherub had a crucial role to play in Ginger's plans to prove to Clyde that Cass could talk. But all his plotting nearly came to nothing when, at the last moment, his parents almost decided not to go out for the evening.

Ginger had chosen Friday evening because earlier in the week he'd heard his parents saying they'd both be out. It was not only the monthly meeting of the Newsagents' Federation, which Dad always went to, but Mum was going to the monthly gathering of her National Women's Register group. But neither of his parents was happy about leaving Ginger alone in the house after the fire. Especially as, the day before, the

Fire Investigation Officer had confirmed that it had been started deliberately.

'But I won't be alone!' Ginger protested. 'Janice'll be here.'

On Friday evenings Janice usually had a crowd of friends in who banished him from the living room. Ginger had banked on that happening this week too, because once she was locked in with her friends she'd neither know, nor care, where he was!

'No she won't,' Mum said, 'the place is in such a mess they're all going to stay the night at Debbie's.'

Ginger's heart sank. After all his scheming! 'But I'll be all right, honestly I will! If anything happens, not that it will,' he added hastily, 'but if it did, there's the phone. I could easily ring for help.'

Mum shook her head. 'I'd feel better if we had neighbours you could contact.'

Ginger shifted anxiously from foot to foot. 'I can always ring the police.'

Dad ignored him. 'It doesn't seem right, leaving him, but this meeting's all about increasing profit margins and I really would like to go.'

'Tonight we're having a book discussion,' Mum said, 'and I've spent the whole of the last month reading a great fat novel so that I could join in.' Mum looked almost as fed-up as Ginger felt. Then she suddenly brightened up. 'I'd forgotten, we're meeting at Val's flat. It's only just across the main road on the new estate. I could give you Val's phone number, then you could ring me there if anything happened and I could be back in five minutes.'

And to Ginger's great relief, this plan was adopted.

9

Car spotting

No sooner were Ginger's parents out of the house, than he began to put his masterplan into action by running down to the churchyard.

He'd only just returned and shut the side door, when Clyde arrived on his bike.

'Are you quite certain you want to go through with this?' Ginger asked.

'Sure, why not?'

'We've never gone to the churchyard at night before and it could be a bit spooky.'

'Nah!' Clyde said scornfully. 'I don't believe in ghosts and all that stuff!'

'Whatever you say, but I'm taking a torch, just in case.'

But even Ginger began to have second thoughts as they passed under the crumbling arch and the rusty wrought-iron gate squealed shut behind them.

It was late November. The moon kept disappearing behind angry lumps of cloud and there was a chill wind blowing which made the branches of the trees sway and sent flurries of crisp, dead leaves clattering along the path behind them.

Several times on their way to the tree house, to Clyde's amusement, Ginger hastily swept the beam of the torch over the dark shapes of the surrounding bushes.

'You are jumpy tonight,' Clyde said with a laugh, as he shinned up the knotted rope into the tree house.

Ginger felt a good deal safer once they were inside and could haul up the rope, making the tree house almost as secure as a castle with a raised drawbridge.

Although the leaves of the fir kept some of the wind off, the wind made the branches sway in the breeze. Ginger thought that it must be like being perched in the crow's nest at the top of a mast of an old sailing ship. They pulled aside the piece of old shower curtain which hung over the window that overlooked the waste ground. Ginger sat on an upturned milk crate, while Clyde perched on the oil drum.

After only twenty minutes they were already beginning to feel cold. Besides which, as Clyde said, 'This is boring!'

'Have some chocolate,' Ginger suggested, pulling a bar from his anorak pocket and snapping four pieces for his pal.

While he was chewing, Clyde said, 'I bet you never saw a car.'

'I did.'

'Well, there's no sign of one now and we could be sitting up here for days without seeing anything.'

'Let's give it another ten minutes,' Ginger said, anxiously peering at the illuminated dial of his watch.

'Five,' said Clyde.

'Ten!' Ginger tried to bargain.

'If nothing happens in five minutes I'm packing it in,' Clyde said firmly.

Ginger was busy trying to think of some delaying tactic he could use, when he heard a car turn off the main road and slow down.

Ginger and Clyde peered out of the window, trying to make out the colour and shape of the car which was parking at the top of the waste ground.

Clyde murmured, 'What colour did you say the car you saw was?'

'Grey, I think. What colour do you think that one is?'

'Bit hard to say, parked under the yellow street lights, it could be yellow, but it might as easily be white, or grey. Hang on, they've switched their lights off and they're getting out.'

Ginger, who'd never really expected there to be a car, began to take more interest. 'They're heading this way.'

The figures crept along in the shadow of the back walls of the old houses but, as they crossed the open ground towards the churchyard wall, the cloud drifted clear of the moon and just for a fleeting moment, Ginger saw the clear silhouettes of two men – one large, the other small. Just the way Dad had described the two men who'd threatened him.

'Get down!' Ginger whispered.

'They'll never spot us up here,' Clyde pointed out.

'If you don't keep your voice down they'll *hear* us, never mind see us!' Ginger hissed.

When the two men reached the churchyard wall the big one had no trouble climbing over, but the little one struggled and had to be heaved up by his coat collar.

Once inside, they forced their way through the undergrowth and seemed to be heading straight for the tree up which Ginger and Clyde were hiding.

'Don't make a sound!' Unfortunately Ginger whispered directly into Clyde's ear so that his breath tickled and Clyde burst out giggling. Ginger did his best to muffle the sound by clapping his hand over Clyde's mouth.

'What was that?' a deep voice, immediately beneath the boys' feet, demanded.

'I didn't hear nothing,' came the reply. 'Not frightened are we, a big boy like you?'

''Course not!' the deep voice said, but it sounded shaky to Ginger.

'Come on, let's get up to that shop!'

The two men had only just reached the path when suddenly a loud, dreadful wailing sound filled the air and a pale light bathed the little cherub in a ghostly glow.

'I'm off!' the larger of the two men shouted, as he began to fight his way back through the undergrowth.

'Come back here!' the smaller man shouted. But when the wails were interrupted by a deep evil laugh, he too turned tail and fled towards the wall, stumbling and falling as the hidden brambles snatched at his clothes and tripped him up.

The big man, who'd vaulted over the wall, was charging over the waste ground long before his colleague had reached the edge of the churchyard.

Ginger laughed out loud as he watched the little man, his feet flailing in the air, whining, 'Wait for me!'

Eventually there was a startled cry as the man fell head first over the wall and disappeared from sight. Moments later he was up again and running after his friend.

'Come on!' Ginger said to Clyde. 'I want to try and get their car number.'

But Clyde didn't move and when Ginger flashed the torch over Clyde's face he realised his mate's smile had frozen into a terror-struck leer. He was pointing towards the eerie glow surrounding the cherub, terrified by the agonized wails coming from it.

'Oh, don't worry about that!' Ginger grinned. 'Let's get up there quick before they disappear.'

Ginger dropped the rope and swarmed down it. Clyde, scared of being left alone, was forced to follow, but he was amazed to see Ginger heading straight for the cherub, calling out, 'Okay, you can stop now!'

Abruptly the hideous mixture of wailing and laughing ceased, though the ghostly light still glowed around the cherub.

'Thank goodness for that!' said a voice.

'You got the timing dead right,' Ginger said.

'You pre-set my timer,' Cass said.

'Who's that?' Clyde asked uncertainly. Although he was relieved the wailing had stopped, he wasn't much happier to be standing in an old graveyard, hearing Ginger carrying on a conversation with an invisible man, particularly one whose voice appeared to be coming up out of the ground!

'It's only Cass,' Ginger said, triumphantly picking up his cassette recorder which he'd brought to the churchyard before Clyde arrived. 'You didn't believe me when I told you he could talk, did you? Now come on, or the car will have gone.'

'You set that up on purpose!' Clyde complained, but Ginger wasn't listening. He was charging up Adventure Street and Clyde had no choice but to follow.

By the time they reached the corner by the shop the car was pulling away.

The men, in their hurry to leave, hadn't bothered to switch on the car's lights and the number on the boot was difficult to read.

'"AJA", I think,' Ginger said, 'but what's the number?'

'"Four, something, something, X."'

But by then the car had turned the corner.

'What were those other numbers?' Ginger demanded.

'I don't know,' Clyde grinned apologetically. 'They could have been noughts, or nines.'

'That's a great help!'

'Or they might have been sixes,' Clyde added helpfully.

10

Closing in

'Why won't you report that car number to the police?' Clyde demanded on Monday when they were back at school.

Ginger had been wondering what to do all weekend. At one point he'd nearly said something to Dad, but Dad was in an even worse mood than usual having had to spend all day Sunday, the only day the shop was shut, redecorating the hall.

'For a start it'd mean admitting to Dad that I was in the churchyard while they were out and we don't even know the car's number, not properly,' Ginger said gloomily. 'Only the letters and one number for sure. We can hardly tell the police AJA four and the rest might be noughts, nines or sixes!'

'We'd have got there sooner if you hadn't been busy showing off your bloomin' cassette recorder,' Clyde grumbled. He still hadn't quite forgiven Ginger for the trick he'd played on him.

'You have to admit it was good though! Cass is brilliant, isn't he?'

'I suppose,' Clyde agreed reluctantly. 'Maybe, if he's so brilliant, he can catch the criminals.'

'I wouldn't be surprised,' Ginger said proudly,

though he had no idea how Cass would do that. 'After all he scared old Crusher off. He still hasn't come back to school.'

Clyde tapped Ginger on the arm and pointed at the figure of a man in a raincoat who was standing across the road from the school, half-hidden by some bushes. 'What do you reckon that bloke's up to?'

'I dunno. Maybe it's one of these weirdos that kidnap kids,' Ginger suggested. 'Do you think we should tell the Head?'

'He's cleared off now anyway,' said Clyde. 'Funny that. He didn't seem much bothered until you looked at him, Ginger. Must be your ugly mug scared him off!'

That morning, a grey car slid to a halt outside Mr Cumpsty's. Two men climbed out and walked into the shop, both wearing crumpled, grey, striped suits.

The shorter of the two men, with a moth-eaten moustache, introduced himself. 'I'm Brent,' he said with an oily smile.

But Mr Cumpsty was nervously looking at Brent's silent partner, a thickset man with a broken nose and eyes as hard and expressionless as black snooker balls. His neck was wider than his head and his enormous fists seemed to hang below his knees.

'My friend and I,' said Brent, 'are very anxious to trace some of our property.'

'Some of *your* property?' Mr Cumpsty was puzzled. 'But I've never seen you before in my life. How could I possibly have anything that belongs to you?'

'Through a little misunderstanding. I lent a valuable piece of equipment to a certain Mr Carter-Symes.'

'Never heard of him,' Mr Cumpsty snapped.

But he rather wished he hadn't been so forceful when the larger man stepped forward and grunted, 'You want to listen good! Brent hadn't finished, had he?'

Mr Cumpsty shrank back. 'Sorry!'

Brent smiled. 'You mustn't mind my friend. Brains is apt to get a bit nervous if he thinks people aren't paying attention. He can be a bit clumsy too, if you know what I mean.'

Mr Cumpsty looked about anxiously. That Ginger boy had done enough damage, he didn't want any more costly accidents. 'What was the name you mentioned?'

'Carter-Symes.'

Mr Cumpsty shook his head. 'But I've never done business with anyone of that name.'

'No,' Brent smiled. 'My boss says you recently received some goods from the bailiff, didn't you?'

'I often do, but I don't see . . .'

'My equipment happened to be in the house of Mr Carter-Symes at the time of the bailiff's visit. It was taken in error and I'd like it back.'

'Yes, he would!' Brains said heavily.

'You'd have to talk to the bailiffs about that. I bought the goods in good faith. If there's anything wrong they'd have to sort that out.'

Brains dropped a heavy fist on the counter making the contents, including a small china bell, rattle. 'I'll sort you out in a minute!'

'Now, Brains, we mustn't be hasty!' Brent reached up to put a pale hand on one of Brain's enormous shoulders. To Mr Cumpsty it looked rather like a moth trying to restrain a mad dog. Brent revealed a set of yellow teeth as he smiled encouragingly at Mr Cumpsty. 'I'm sure we won't have to bother the bailiffs about this little matter. You see, I'm quite happy to buy the goods back.' Brent slipped a crocodile-skin wallet from his inside pocket and opened it on the counter, revealing a wad of notes. Although Mr Cumpsty could only see their edges, his practised eyes immediately recognised the twenty-pound notes.

Rubbing his hands greedily, Mr Cumpsty's attitude changed completely. 'That's different! Quite different! I thought you were implying I had stolen goods in the shop, which might mean involving the police.'

Brains shot a startled glance over his shoulder. 'Police, where?'

'Calm down, Brains,' Brent said soothingly and turning to Mr Cumpsty he added, 'The police bother Brains. You see, he gets a lot of parking tickets.'

'Oh, yes.' Mr Cumpsty couldn't imagine anyone having the courage to give Brains a parking ticket, but he was anxious to get the two men out of his shop as soon as possible. 'What exactly was it you were looking for?'

'A cassette recorder.'

'Oh, I've plenty of those, you'd have to describe it.'

'This one is very recognisable. About the size of a cornflakes packet, it's grey, with a display panel on the front.'

The colour drained out of Mr Cumpsty's face until it would have matched the recorder, if it had still been in the shop. 'But I've sold it.'

'What?' shrieked the little man. 'Who to?'

'A boy came in and bought it. At least, he gave me a pound for it because it didn't work.'

Brent couldn't believe his ears. 'A pound! You sold it for a pound?'

Mr Cumpsty watched the man snapping the wallet shut. It felt as if he was experiencing a total eclipse of the sun. 'I'm sure I could get it back and sell it to you.'

Brains pushed his bruised face close to Mr Cumpsty's. 'We don't deal with middle men. We like things straight from the horse's mouth – like fresh spit!'

Ignoring Brains, Brent demanded, 'What's this boy's name?'

'I get hundreds of them poking about in here, I don't know all their names.'

'What *do* you know about him then?'

'He has red hair and he lives at the newsagent's on the corner of Adventure Street.'

Brent's mouth opened wide in astonishment and he tapped Brains on the arm. 'Now, there's coincidence.'

Brains looked around him. 'Where?'

'That's where the Nutts live.'

'I thought nuts lived in trees,' Brains muttered.

'MR NUTT! You remember Mr Nutt, don't you, Brains?'

Light dawned very slowly on his battered face like a car headlight approaching through thick fog. 'Oh, yes.'

'I think it's time we paid the Nutts another visit.'

'Yes,' Brains licked his lips. 'Kill two birds with one stone.'

'Quiet, Brains!' Brent gave one last oily smile to Mr

Cumpsty. 'Thanks for your help. I hope we shan't have to trouble you again.'

Brent turned to leave, but Brains was still leaning on the counter, leering at Mr Cumpsty. 'We don't like having to do things twice. Makes me very nervous.' Brains picked up the tiny china bell from the counter and shook it amazingly gently. 'Pretty little thing, isn't it?'

'Yes,' Mr Cumpsty agreed hastily.

Brains dropped the delicate bell on to the floor and stamped on it, grinding his heel on the broken bits until he'd reduced them to a fine powder.

It was long after they'd gone, when Mr Cumpsty had recovered enough to make a cup of strong tea to steady his nerves, that he remembered the young man who'd come into the shop last week. He had also asked about the same cassette recorder, though in a pleasanter manner!

Mr Cumpsty thoughtfully rubbed his stubbly chin. 'Why all this sudden interest in one machine, especially when it doesn't work!' But that didn't stop him writing a sign in spidery felt-tip which he hung in the window:

'CASSETTE RECORDERS URGENTLY
NEEDED. GOOD PRICES PAID.'

Clyde and Ginger were just leaving the main gates after school, when Ginger felt a hand grab the strap of his school bag and try to pull it off his shoulder.

'Give over!' he said. He twisted round, expecting one of Crusher's mafia but was amazed to find it was the man in the shabby raincoat, the one Clyde had spotted watching them earlier. Ginger tucked the bag firmly under his arm. 'Here, what's your game?' he demanded.

The man, who was in his late twenties, blinked his pale blue eyes at Ginger through steel-rimmed spectacles. 'I . . . er . . . I . . . ,' the man's mouth opened and closed like a stranded fish, '. . . thought you were somebody else,' he muttered and then turned and ran off.

At first the two boys were too surprised to give chase and when they did there was no sign of him.

'I bet that's another of the gang,' Ginger said. 'While Abbott and Costello are setting fire to the shop, he's tailing me. I tell you, things are beginning to hot up!'

11

Under attack

Just before six, when Ginger returned from his paper round, he was amazed to find the shop in darkness and the door locked.

'Dad never shuts the shop until gone six,' he muttered to himself. But not only was the side door locked too, but there was no reply when he banged on it with his fist. 'Nobody said anything about going out.'

Using the spare key he kept on a cord round his neck, Ginger let himself in and switched on the hall light. He was surrounded by the sickly smell of new paint.

'Anybody home?' he called out hopefully, though with the whole house cloaked in silent darkness, he knew it was a fairly stupid question.

Making sure he locked the door behind him and switching on every light he passed, Ginger made his way to the kitchen. There were no comforting smells of cooking and without much hope he peered into the oven which was cold and empty.

He poured himself a glass of milk and opened the biscuit box. Inside was a note from Mum.

Dear Ginger,

Thought this would be the first place you went!

Janice had an accident at school and they've taken her up to the hospital for a check-up and they're going to do some X-rays. So Dad and I have gone up there. I don't know how long we'll be. Sorry about tea – we'll get some fish and chips on the way home. Don't finish *all* the biscuits before we get back and Dad says you're not to raid the chocolate in the shop!

Keep ALL the doors locked and don't let *anyone* in.

Love,
Mum.

He'd hardly finished reading the note when somebody knocked loudly on the shop door.

Thinking it might be a customer as surprised as he was to find the shop closed, Ginger went into the darkened shop and stood behind the counter.

'Come on, Mr Nutt,' called a voice. 'It's no good hiding. We've seen the lights, so we know you're in there.'

Projected on to the glass door by the street lights, Ginger saw two shadows, one small and one large and he recognised the voice as belonging to the shorter of the two men he'd seen creeping through the churchyard.

'I'm not standing out here all night,' the man went on.

'Shall I break the door down, boss?' the second man asked, thumping the door hard with his closed fist to back up the suggestion. The reinforced glass shuddered under the impact.

'Now, Brains, we don't want to go smashing up the happy home!' the little man said. 'After all, it'll soon be ours! There'll be no need for violence if Mr Nutt will be sensible and open up the door, so that we can have a little chat. Can you hear me, Mr Nutt?'

Thinking it would get rid of them, Ginger shouted back, 'Go away, he's not here!'

'Oh.' The little man pressed his nose against the glass and peered into the darkened shop, shielding his eyes with his hand to get rid of the reflections caused by the street lights.

'Would that be Master Nutt? The one with red hair who bought a cassette recorder off Mr Cumpsty?'

Ginger was startled. These men seemed to know everything!

'I'd like a word with you. So open up the door, there's a good little fellow.'

Ginger ground his teeth. He hated being referred to as a 'little fellow', almost as much as Mum resented being called Dad's 'good lady'! He shouted back defiantly. 'I'm not opening the door and they won't be back for ages, so you might as well clear off!'

No sooner were the words out than Ginger could have bitten his tongue off!

'Oh, I see!' the oily-voiced man said. Though Ginger couldn't see his face, he knew the man was smiling about as pleasantly as a crocodile that's spotted a hunk of rotting meat. 'If they aren't coming back for a while, I think we might slip back to the office for that set of skeleton keys you've got, Brains, and then we can let ourselves in!'

'Why don't I just smash the door down?'

'Because we don't want the whole world knowing what we're doing and you don't want "Breaking and Entering" added to your crime sheet, along with "Grievous Bodily Harm" and "Malicious Wounding", do you?'

'But it'll still be breaking and entering if I use a skeleton key.'

The little man's patience with his thick partner was wearing thin. 'But if the door isn't damaged we can swear the little fellow invited us in and then who's to know the difference? Now, get in the car! Don't go away, sonny,' he called to Ginger, 'we'll be back very shortly!'

Although he was frightened, Ginger kept his wits about him. This time he made no mistake about the car number. Clyde hadn't been far out. It was AJA 4069 X and Ginger wrote it down on the envelope Dad used for his sums.

That done, his first thought was to make a run for it and get as far away from the shop as possible before the men returned. But as he was about to go towards the door a sudden movement across the road caught his eye. Standing in the shadows of the doorway of one of the empty houses opposite was the man in the raincoat, the one who only hours before had made a grab at him.

'They're working together!' Ginger said triumphantly to himself. 'Smart stuff! They tell me they're leaving and drive off, but the third guy is waiting to pounce the moment I set foot outside. Well, they're not going to catch me that easily.'

His next thought, now that he knew the whole of the car number, was to call the police. But apart from the number, what could he tell them? Two men had knocked at the door, asked to speak to his dad and then said they were going to get some skeleton keys.

Ginger could just hear the policeman's reply. 'I think they were just trying to scare you, son. Anyway they've gone away and we can't send cars out on a wild-goose chase. You give us another ring if they do come back and we'll be round like a shot.'

Maybe he ought to try to ring his parents at the hospital, but he didn't really know which department they'd be in and he might waste valuable time, being transferred between Casualty and X-ray, without ever finding them.

Clyde was his only hope!

Ginger dived into the hall, picked up the phone and rang the number. He just hoped Clyde hadn't suddenly taken it into his head to go out to the cinema, or a disco.

Clyde's mum answered and much to Ginger's relief, instantly put Clyde on the line.

'Clyde, there's nobody in the house but me and those two blokes we saw in the churchyard have been knocking on the door. Get on your bike and get down here as fast as you can.'

'I could be twenty minutes,' Clyde warned him.

'Do it in ten if you can!' Ginger said and then, as an afterthought, he added, 'And when you get here, make sure you go down the entry and come in by the back door.'

Unfortunately, Clyde had already put the phone down and left home before Ginger could finish his sentence.

Ginger raced round the house collecting up a few things he needed, determined that even if the men returned before Clyde arrived, they would find he was more than ready for them.

12

Traps for boobies

'Ouch!' yelled Clyde from outside the side door.

'Hang on a minute,' Ginger called out. He carefully detached The Super Electric Handshocker he'd wired up to the metal handle and unlocked the door to let in Clyde. 'I warned you to use the back door!'

'I never heard you,' Clyde rubbed his hand. Fortunately he'd only touched the handle lightly and suffered more from surprise than injury. 'What was that?'

Ginger twisted the wires of the handshocker back round the door handle and switched it on again. 'Just a surprise I lined up for our friends, in case they're stupid enough to try to break in! Let's go down to the cellar.'

'What for?'

'To switch off the main fusebox so they won't be able to use the lights. I waited until you arrived in case you fell over something.' Ginger didn't admit that he hadn't been able to stomach the idea of facing the two men alone in the dark. Now that Clyde had arrived he felt far more confident.

Once the house was plunged into darkness, Ginger

led the way by torch light up to his room, warning Clyde to watch his step.

They'd just reached Ginger's room when they heard furious banging on the shop door. Getting no reply, the men went round to the side of the house and hammered on that door instead.

'I'll give you one more chance,' Brent shouted. 'If you don't let us in, we'll use our skeleton keys to come in anyway but it'll be the worse for you.'

'I hope we're doing the right thing,' Ginger whispered to his mate, who was crouched with him on the floor by Ginger's bed.

''Course you are!' Clyde murmured.

'You ready, Cass? You know what to do?'

'Just say the word,' Cass shouted back, from his position under the bed, with an accompanying flicker of his green and yellow lights.

'Ssh!' hissed Ginger.

'*You* set my volume,' Cass said accusingly.

'That's for later, this is now! We'd better keep as quiet as possible so that we can hear what they're up to.'

'There's no pleasing some people!' Cass grumbled before he lapsed into silence.

Ginger could just make out the sound of somebody fiddling with the lock of the side door. 'Here we go!' he muttered.

There was a loud cry of protest from Brains as he firmly gripped the door handle to open the door and got the full charge from Ginger's handshocker!

'Don't mess about, Brains!' the unsympathetic Brent said. 'Let's have some lights on.'

Clyde gleefully dug Ginger in the ribs when they heard the men stumbling about in the hall followed by the fruitless jiggling of light switches.

'Power must be off. Perhaps they haven't paid their bill. Did you bring a torch?' Brent asked crossly.

'No, but I've got a cigarette lighter.'

'Then get it out, you great pudding!' Brent said irritably.

Peering under the bed and out through his open bedroom door, Ginger saw a pale flickering light coming from the direction of the hall.

Brent called out. 'It's no good hiding, it's only a matter of time before we find you.'

'And the longer it takes, the sorrier you'll be when we *do*!' Brains added menacingly.

Getting no reply, Brent hastily pushed open the sitting-room door and jumped back as a bag fell, thumped Brains on the head hard enough to burst and smothered them in flour.

It was another of the series of traps Ginger had hastily prepared.

They opened the kitchen door more carefully, but not carefully enough to stop the precariously balanced plastic bucket of water pouring down over them. The water instantly mixed with the flour to turn it into a gooey paste which rapidly ran down their faces on to their clothes.

'My threads are ruined!' Brains roared, scraping off some of the sludge and flicking it angrily at the kitchen wall.

'This isn't funny, kid!' Brent shouted. 'You'd better come out before Brains gets *really* mad.'

'You'll have to find me first!' Ginger shouted back defiantly.

'Upstairs!' Brains shouted and set off with Brent following close behind.

Brains had run up six steps before the stair carpet, from which Ginger had removed all the rods which held it, slipped from under his feet. As he fell, the cigarette lighter flew out of his hand, plunging them into darkness. Brains fell back on Brent, knocking him over and they found themselves lying on top of each other at the bottom of the staircase in a bruised, tangled heap.

Ginger and Clyde collapsed in laughter as they heard Brent's muffled voice protesting, 'Get off me, you great lump!'

After a great deal of argument, the men retrieved the lost lighter and the boys' laughter died away as Brains shouted, 'I'm going to get you for that!' His huge feet sounded very menacing as he stamped his way up the bare, wooden steps of the staircase.

'Come on!' Ginger said to Clyde.

They raced out on to the landing with a full carrier bag, leant over the banisters and pelted the two crooks with a hail of water bombs.

'Right that does it!' Brains bellowed.

But just as he reached the top step, his foot caught under a tripwire of fishing line which sent him sprawling headlong, until finally his head hit the wall with a terrific crack.

Even that didn't stop Brains. If anything it made him even angrier and more determined. 'Come here, you little brat!' he growled.

Staggering to his feet, Brains launched himself at Ginger, who was waiting in the doorway of his room. All Brains' weight went on the end of a board Ginger had loosened by removing the screws. One end of the plank flew up and smashed into Brains' face.

Again Brains' cigarette lighter went out, there was a brief howl of pain and, as the two boys raced back to the bedroom, they heard the stunned Brains slump to the floor.

'Brains!' Brent shouted, cautiously feeling his way up the stairs. 'Don't muck about! Put the light back on. Where are you, Brains?'

Ginger waited until Brent sounded as if he was almost at the top of the stairs before he hissed, 'Now, Cass!'

Cass burst into life producing a barrage of sound. First there was a police car, complete with siren, which appeared to be screeching to a halt outside the house. Doors slammed and men shouted, 'We've got you surrounded. You might as well give yourselves up!'

Brent turned and fled, as fast as possible, back down the pitch-dark staircase, completely forgetting the pile of crumpled carpet waiting for him at the bottom.

He tripped, fell, smashed his head against the wall and lay still.

'Okay, Cass, that's enough!' Ginger shouted above the uproar.

'Thank goodness.' Cass's voice seemed to be getting curiously deeper. 'My batteries are failing fast.'

Grabbing Cass, Ginger ran out on to the landing with Clyde, whooping, 'We've done it!'

He flashed his torch over the two unconscious figures. 'You tie them up while I ring for the police,' he said, handing Clyde a length of washing line.

Clyde was finishing the last knot as Ginger returned. 'There wasn't enough rope to do Brains properly,' he explained, 'so I've taken the belt off his trousers as well.'

Brent was coming round. 'What hit me?' he muttered and then, realising he'd been trussed up like a Christmas turkey, he began to struggle. 'Here, son, let me out of this,' he pleaded. 'We were only having a little joke. You know we wouldn't really hurt you.'

'You can tell that to the police!' Ginger replied and ran down to the cellar to switch the lights back on.

But as Ginger came back up from the cellar, he almost went into orbit. Standing in the open front door was the man in the raincoat.

'Oh, no!' Ginger groaned. 'I'd forgotten you were lurking about on the other side of the road! But you're too late, I've already phoned the police and they're on their way.'

'Police?' The young man blinked through his steel-rimmed glasses, trying to take in the scene. On a pile of carpet, at the foot of the stairs, sat a bewildered little man, tied up with washing line, whose wet suit was smeared with what looked like thin, grey porridge. 'What on earth's happened to him?'

'He's with you, isn't he?' Ginger asked, jerking a thumb towards Brent.

'No, certainly not,' the young man said. 'Though I do know him, of course,' he admitted.

'Aha! I thought as much,' Ginger said triumphantly.

The young man nodded eagerly. 'Oh, yes, we're both after the same thing.'

'I know, you all want our shop, don't you?'

The man looked baffled. 'Your shop? No, certainly not. I want my cassette recorder.'

It was Ginger's turn to be surprised. 'Cass?'

'At last!' Cass sighed in his newly acquired deep voice, which was getting deeper by the second as his batteries ran down. He just managed to say, 'Carter-Symes, please take me away from this mad housssse . . . !' before his motor stopped and he fell silent.

13

A not so happy ending

'Gin-ger!'

Dad, with Mum and Janice, had let himself in through the shop and had almost fallen over the trussed-up figure of Brent. 'What's he doing tied up like that?' But Dad's face grew redder with anger as he took in the mess all over his newly-redecorated hall. Flour spilled out from the sitting room, there was a soaked floor and a bucket by the kitchen door and the stair carpet was in a heap at the foot of the stairs.

'What on earth's been going on here?' Then he saw Clyde and last of all, Carter-Symes. 'And who the hell are you?'

Ginger saw the disappointed look on Mum's face and the 'You're-really-in-for-it-now!' smirk spreading across Janice's face, but his explanation was delayed by the noisy arrival of a police car, a real one this time!

One of the policemen stayed with Brent while the other took everyone else into the kitchen for an explanation. Ginger and Clyde's story lasted a long time, with frequent sidetracks to include Mr Cumpsty and what had happened in the churchyard.

The only part everyone found hard to swallow, just

as Clyde had, was when Ginger started to explain that his new cassette recorder could think and talk, as well as make noises.

'A likely story!' Janice said scornfully.

'Oh, yes?' Ginger retorted. 'Well, listen to this!' He pressed down the Pause button, which was usually enough to activate Cass. 'Show them what you can do, Cass!'

Silence, except for a stifled giggle from Janice.

'Cass! It's not a secret any more,' Ginger insisted. 'Tell them who you are!'

'Come on, son,' Mr Nutt said, putting his arm round Ginger's shoulders. 'You've done a grand job, you and Clyde, but don't over-egg the pudding.'

'But it's true!' Ginger protested. Then he remembered what was wrong. 'I'd forgotten, his batteries have run down.'

As Ginger fumbled with the case to the battery compartment Janice said, 'Pull the other one, it's got bells on it!'

'He is telling the truth,' Carter-Symes, who had ended up in a corner perched, almost out of sight, on an upturned washing basket, added quietly, but everybody ignored him.

But even leaving out the possibility of a talking tape recorder, faced with the very real evidence of two crooks bound up in washing line, the policemen needed little convincing as to what had been going on.

'Mr Nutt,' the policeman said, 'we'll get these two villains down to the station and then tomorrow, when they've calmed down a bit, you can bring these lads along so they can make a proper statement.'

‘I’ll get even with you for this!’ Brent hissed at the Nutts as he was led out to the car.

‘After what you’ve been up to,’ the policeman warned him, ‘the only thing you’ll be getting even with, for a few years, is sewing a pile of mailbags, in jail!’

Brains, who’d still been unconscious when Clyde removed his belt, made the mistake of angrily waving his arms about and made a very undignified exit, his trousers round his knees, displaying Bart Simpson boxer shorts!

‘Clyde,’ Mr Nutt said, ‘you’d better be off too, your mum’ll be worried. But thanks for helping Ginger out.’

‘Yes, thanks for coming over, mate!’ Ginger slapped Clyde on the back. ‘I could never have done it without you.’

‘Wait ’til we tell them at school,’ Clyde said, with a grin so broad it almost split his face from ear to ear.

As Ginger shut the door he happened to glance at Janice and suddenly remembered her accident. Strangely, apart from a bruise on the forehead, she looked perfectly all right. ‘I thought you were supposed to be dying or something?’

‘I slipped at school and knocked myself out. It was nothing but the Head sent me to hospital.’

‘So that’s all right,’ Mum said, ‘but the fish and chips we brought with us are spoiling in the oven, so we’d better eat before we start tidying up.’

‘That’s very kind of you,’ a voice said and the four astonished Nutts turned to find Carter-Symes still in the kitchen.

'Good heavens,' said Dad, 'I'd forgotten all about you.'

Ginger hadn't. He knew only too well why Carter-Symes was there and he wasn't looking forward to this part of the evening.

'Where do you fit into all this rigmarole?' Dad asked.

'If this is going to be another long story,' Mum said, 'I think we'd best eat while you tell it.'

'I'm afraid so,' apologised Carter-Symes.

'Never mind,' Mum said brightly, laying an extra place, 'there's plenty for five.'

And so, over their meal, the whole history of the invention and loss of the Carter-Symes 2000 was told. Several times laden forks hovered before open mouths and in the end Carter-Symes decided the easiest way was to demonstrate and fresh batteries were inserted. Which only made the story longer, because Cass kept interrupting and Janice insisted on asking Carter-Symes to get Cass to do the same thing over and over again.

But Ginger guessed it wasn't Cass she was going gooey over. He'd noticed the odd way she'd been looking at Carter-Symes from the moment he removed his glasses and flicked back his thick, blond hair.

'So you see, Ginger,' Carter-Symes finished, 'it *is* absolutely vital that I have the 2000 back again.'

'But I bought him, he's mine,' Ginger defiantly replied. Deep down he knew he was going to be forced to hand Cass over, but he wasn't going to give him up without a fuss.

'I tell you what, Ginger,' Carter-Symes suggested,

'I'll give you twice what you paid for him.'

'Two pounds! Cass is worth far more than that to me.'

'And to me too. He represents not only twelve years' work, but possibly my entire future as well.'

'Ginger, don't be so stingy,' Janice sneered.

'I suppose you wouldn't like another bang on the head?' Ginger said.

'Gin-ger!' Mum cautioned him.

'Look, Ginger,' Dad said quietly, 'I know how you feel, but this is Mr Carter-Symes' livelihood you're talking about. Put it this way: it would be just as if you'd stood back and let those crooks wreck our shop and put us out of business. You wouldn't have done that, would you?'

'Of course not but think what might have happened here tonight if I hadn't had Cass to help,' Ginger pointed out.

'Exactly,' Dad said. 'And that's why we ought to show our gratitude and let Mr Carter-Symes have his recorder back.'

'I wish you'd all stop calling him "it"; he's Cass.'

'Only because that's what you called me,' Cass interrupted.

'I thought you were getting to like the name,' Ginger said.

'Well, yes,' Cass admitted, 'I did eventually and it's certainly better than being just a number.'

'And we had some exciting times together,' Ginger insisted.

'True,' Cass agreed, 'if anything a little too exciting for my taste!'

But Dad wasn't listening, his mind was already made up. 'So that's settled.'

Ginger nodded gloomily, though he brightened up a little when Carter-Symes gave him a ten-pound note instead of the two pounds he'd originally suggested, adding, 'I promise as soon as they're manufactured, you shall have the very first one off the production line, for free. In the meantime, perhaps when I get settled into my new place you'd like to come round?'

'I'd love to,' Janice said, fluttering her eyelashes at him.

But Carter-Symes, who didn't seem to notice, carried on talking to Ginger. 'I could show you some of the other inventions.'

'Though none are quite as impressive as me!' Cass insisted, but he shut down in a huff when everyone laughed.

'Apple pie, anyone?' Mum suggested. 'Though I'm afraid there's only cold custard to go with it.'

'That's very kind of you,' Carter-Symes said, picking up Cass, 'but I really should be going.'

After he'd gone and they'd cleared up the house a bit, Ginger went upstairs to bed. Considering Cass's compact size, Ginger's room seemed surprisingly empty without him. He really missed having him to talk to and knew it would be a long time before he got over the loss.

He was thinking back through the adventures he'd shared with Cass, when he heard his sister thumping up the stairs, still angry that Carter-Symes had almost ignored her.

Seconds later Janice let out a blood-curdling scream.

'Oh, dear!' Ginger giggled to himself.

Janice threw open his door. 'Ginger, I'll kill you for this!' she yelled.

But Ginger doubled up with laughter at the sight of the cold custard, which Mum thought was in the fridge but which Ginger had put above Janice's door for the crooks, trickling down through her hair!

14

Not quite the end

After the kick they'd got out of telling everyone at school about the break-in and capturing the crooks, life suddenly seemed very dull to Ginger and Clyde.

Once the story appeared in the newspapers curiosity brought the shop some new customers. Then the Nutts heard that the property company had sold all the houses they'd bought and the plans for the development had been dropped.

In fact three couples had already moved back into their old homes.and several more people had been to look at the others, so Dad decided it would be well worthwhile keeping the business.

But Ginger wasn't keen. He thought Adventure Street had had all the adventures it was likely to get.

It was a few days before Christmas when Carter-Symes phoned Ginger and invited him round.

'You can bring a friend too, if you like,' he'd said.

To Janice's intense annoyance, Ginger had naturally chosen to take Clyde with him.

Though it was all very interesting, especially the automatic fish-feeder and a device for trimming finger-nails, which consisted of a kind of mechanical glove,

Ginger agreed with what Cass had said, there was nothing as exciting as him. To make matters worse, Cass wasn't available for conversation, he was lying in bits on the work bench.

'I'm in the middle of some modifications at the moment,' Carter-Symes apologised.

Ginger felt like somebody visiting a sick relative in hospital.

'But there is a company definitely interested in marketing him now,' Carter-Symes added. 'So you may not have to wait too long before you have one of your own!'

'Thank you,' Ginger said, but in a funny kind of way he knew it would never be the same as owning the original Cass.

Carter-Symes sensed Ginger's disappointment and, anxious to make it up to him, he took from a shelf a digital watch, which he dusted off on the seat of his trousers and gave to Ginger. 'Why don't you have this? A sort of early Christmas present.'

Ginger thanked him and strapped the watch on to his wrist. 'Did you make it?' he asked hopefully.

'No, I didn't. It was made by an old man I met at an inventors' convention. He gave it to me to try and sell the idea for him, but shortly afterwards he died and I couldn't trace any relatives, so I kept it.'

'Thanks very much,' Ginger said. It was very nice, but not nearly as exciting, or as useful, as Cass.

Carter-Symes pointed to a gold button on the side of the large watch face. 'To be honest I never have found out what that does.'

After big slices of chocolate cake and glasses of ice-cream soda, Ginger and Clyde thanked Carter-Symes and left.

Although it was dark and cold, Ginger cheered up a little when he noticed a new sign hanging in Mr Cumpsty's lit window.

'NO CASSETTE RECORDERS BOUGHT'

Beneath it, the window was crammed full with all the machines Mr Cumpsty had been forced to buy, but of course, not the one he'd really wanted to get his hands on!

'Nice of Carter-Symes to give you that watch,' Clyde said.

'I suppose,' Ginger said, 'but I've already got a watch.'

'You could always sell it to Mr Cumpsty,' Clyde suggested.

'I could.' Ginger peered at the watch and started to fiddle with the various buttons. Illuminated figures changed and alarms buzzed, but nothing out of the ordinary happened. 'I wonder what this one does?' Ginger said, pressing the gold button Carter-Symes had pointed out.

To Clyde's amazement, Ginger instantly slumped down to the pavement.

'Ginger, what's up?' Clyde shook Ginger but, although he could see Ginger was still breathing, there was no response. 'That's weird! He's fast asleep! Now, that's what I call a snooze alarm!'

But there was rather more to it than that!

15

Out for the count

Ginger's stomach trailed so far behind him he could easily have been plummeting twenty floors down a lift shaft. It combined the horrifying falling sensation he'd often suffered in nightmares with being fired from a cannon down a cold, dark, tunnel into the teeth of a hurricane. But usually he woke quickly from nightmares, whereas now he seemed to be on a crazy, white-knuckle ride, whooshing endlessly through space.

Ginger's ears popped so hard he was scared the drums would burst. His face felt so distorted by the unseen G-force that he was terrified his eyeballs would be sucked out of their sockets and the flesh stripped from his cheekbones.

When he did manage, briefly, to open his eyes, brilliant pinpricks of light hurtled towards him and were transformed into huge, vividly coloured meteorites which forced him to duck as they noisily flashed by him.

Abruptly he collided with an invisible wall.

Stunned by the impact, Ginger's head whirled, but through the buzzing in his ears, he thought he heard a man shouting.

'Clear the way!'

Ginger didn't know what had happened to him. His head was still spinning as he picked himself up. Only the honking horn pulled him round in time to avoid being run down by a noisy, smelly vintage car being driven by a man dressed in flying helmet and goggles. Beside the driver sat a woman. Her large, lavender-coloured hat was held on by a scarf tied in a bow beneath her chin and trimmed with a large feather. A matching veil hid her face.

Ginger wondered what had happened to Clyde. He was still very confused. In the half-light it was difficult to see and his imagination seemed to be playing tricks on him, but the buildings still seemed oddly familiar.

He struggled to sort out exactly what had happened and began to think that perhaps all the flashing lights were part of some terrible accident. Maybe he'd had a bump on the head which had caused him to lose his memory.

'But if I've lost my memory,' he mumbled to himself, 'why do I remember I'm Ginger?'

A hoarse voice interrupted his thoughts. 'You ought to be more careful. Those contraptions come up on you like the devil himself.'

Ginger hadn't noticed he was standing next to a barefoot, grubby boy of about his own age, who was all in rags.

'Are they off to a fancy dress ball?' Ginger asked.

The boy looked puzzled. 'No, why?'

Ginger laughed. 'Well, you've got to admit their clothes are a bit weird!'

'Not really,' the boy replied.

Ginger glanced down and discovered that his own bare legs stuck out of a pair of grey flannel shorts like two skinny sticks of celery. Worse, his trendy trainers had disappeared and been replaced with black lace-up shoes! Ginger had never dressed like this, not even at primary school!

The only thing he was wearing which he recognised was the watch Carter-Symes had given him.

'What's going on?' Ginger wondered out loud.

'Well, Jack,' the boy said helpfully, 'I'm off home to see if there's anything left for me tea. I don't suppose you could spare a copper or two? A drop of beer might ease me dad's temper.'

Ginger stuffed his hands deep into his pockets and was surprised to discover he had got money. Though on closer inspection it looked more like a useless collection of foreign coins. 'It's all I've got,' he apologised.

'All? There's enough pennies and ha'pennies there, not to mention that silver thre'penny piece and them farthings, to pay our rent for the week.'

Ginger laughed scornfully. 'Farthings! What's a farthing?'

The boy stared at Ginger as if he'd grown a spare head. 'Don't they teach you nothing at that posh school of yours? A farthing's a quarter of a penny, isn't it?'

Ginger didn't stop laughing. 'You couldn't buy anything with a quarter of a penny!'

'Step inside this shop and I'll soon show you!' the boy said jerking his thumb at the building behind them.

Ginger realised they were standing outside a strangely familiar shop. It looked a little rather like Mr Cumpsty's, except this window, lit by flickering yellow gas jets, displayed groceries. Some of the goods Ginger recognised, like the jars of Bovril, though there was something wrong about the printing of the label.

'Come on, Jack!' the boy said eagerly and before Ginger could stop him, he'd opened the door and tugged Ginger inside.

The shop, dimly lit by a single gas lamp hanging from the low ceiling, smelled strongly of soap, cheese and bacon. Large containers, labelled raisins and cocoa, were ranged across shelves. A massive polished mahogany counter supported a huge set of brass scales and an enormous till. In front of the counter, on the sawdust-strewn, wood-block floor, stood fat hessian sacks full of things like flour and dried peas.

Hanging on the wall Ginger spotted a calendar which was open at December 1913.

Suddenly everything clicked.

He must have had an accident during a school trip, like the visit to a Victorian school. They'd had to dress up in daft clothes like these and sit at uncomfortable desks, writing on slates, while this bloke pretended to be a stern, old-fashioned schoolmaster.

Relieved he'd sorted things out, Ginger wasn't at all surprised when a man with side whiskers and wearing a large white apron, appeared behind the counter and said, with quite convincing severity, 'Now, Will, I've warned you before, no more credit!'

'Me? I'm not expecting tick,' Ginger's companion said.

Ginger smiled, this was no doubt part of the regular performance for each school party. Ginger couldn't help wondering where the rest of his class were. He wished he was with them.

Will explained. 'My friend Jack's got cash.'

Only Monopoly money, Ginger thought, and why does he keep calling me Jack? Maybe it's a name he uses for everyone, like Glaswegians are supposed to call every man Jimmy!

'Ah well, that's different,' the man said, 'but young Alice will have to serve you, I'm busy stocktaking.'

Alice was a pretty girl, rather older than the boys. Like Ginger, she too had red hair, though hers was carefully bunched in ringlets and held back from her face by a turquoise clip. She had a rosebud mouth and bright blue eyes. Over her dress she wore a spotless white smock and she spoke shyly. 'Yes, please, can I help you?'

Ginger realised he was thirsty. 'I don't suppose you've got one, but what I'd really like is a can of Coke.'

The girl, who was obviously as good an actress as the others, pretended to look mystified. 'You know we don't sell coke here. You can buy it from the Gaslight Company down by the canal.'

'Don't waste time on daft jokes, Jack,' Will said. 'I'm starving! Alice, let's have a quarter of broken biscuits.'

Alice came round the counter and from one of the glass-fronted boxes, she filled a paper bag with a mixture of broken biscuits, carefully weighing them on the brass scales. 'That's a penny, please,' she said.

Will rudely snatched the bag off her and busily stuffed his face, but Ginger was getting bored. 'This is all very well, but I've got to go and find my mates. It's late and I'll get in trouble if I miss the bus and they go back without me.'

Will wasn't sure what was happening, but determined not to lose the biscuits, dived out of the shop.

When Ginger tried to follow, Alice called to the grocer, who shot nimbly round the counter and grabbed Ginger by the wrist. 'Now then, young Jack! What's all this – trying to run off without paying, eh?'

'My name's not Jack and I've got to find my friends!' Ginger insisted.

'One of your friends,' the man said heavily, 'has just run off with a bag of biscuits and you're staying here until they're paid for, even if you are family.'

'Ouch!' Ginger cried out. 'You're hurting my wrist!'

The grocer gripped him so fiercely that Ginger felt his watch biting into his flesh.

'I'll hurt you all right!' the grocer said. 'I don't take kindly to thieves, especially when they make themselves out to be toffs as can easily afford to pay for what they want! Now, either you pay up and look pleasant, or I lock you up in the back and send for the police!'

The grocer tightened his grip even more until Ginger howled with pain and then suddenly blacked out.

'What's up with you?' Clyde asked.

Ginger was sitting on the pavement next to Clyde. As the truth began to dawn, he scrambled to his feet. 'Clyde,' he burbled, 'you'll never guess what just happened to me.'

'I *know* what happened,' Clyde said. 'One minute we were walking along the pavement and the next you'd fainted.'

'No, I didn't,' Ginger yelled excitedly at Clyde. 'I've been on a journey back in time! That's why I'm wearing these stupid clothes.'

'You ain't been nowhere and you always wear stupid clothes!'

Ginger looked down and discovered he was back in his jeans and trainers. Even the money in his pocket had changed back to modern coins.

The full truth hit Ginger with the force of a bolt of lightning!

'It's this watch Carter-Symes gave me! When I pressed the gold button I shot back in time. Carter-Symes didn't know what it was for. Well, now I do!'

Clyde was about to scoff, until he remembered how they'd fallen out when he wouldn't believe Ginger about Cass. 'But you were only out for a couple of seconds,' he said carefully.

'Really? It seemed longer than that where I was and the only reason I came back was because the grocer accidentally pressed the button.'

'Grocer! What are you on about?' Clyde demanded and Ginger had to explain it all.

When Ginger had finished, Clyde still wasn't sure what to believe. 'But does the watch send you off just anywhere?'

Ginger shrugged. 'Dunno. The shop looked a bit like this one, but the calendar on the wall definitely said 1913.'

'Got it!' said Clyde. 'Look at the time now.'

Ginger couldn't understand what Clyde was getting at. 'Quarter past seven, so what?'

'I thought it was strange when Carter-Symes first showed it us. Your watch shows the time in the figures of the twenty-four-hour clock,' Clyde explained patiently. 'Like now it doesn't say 7.15, it says it's 1915 and it's a couple of minutes since you first pressed that button.'

'I'll try it again to be sure,' Ginger said, completely forgetting how scared he'd been the first time.

'Hang on!' Clyde cried out.

But it was too late. Ginger once more slumped, lifeless, on to the pavement.

16

Timeslip

A woman in a fun-fur coat stopped to peer anxiously at Ginger, who was half-sitting, half-lying against the wall beneath Mr Cumpsty's window.

'Is your little friend all right?'

'Oh, yes,' Clyde grinned happily. 'He keeps doing this.'

'He has gone very pale,' she said doubtfully.

Mr Cumpsty, having ignored Ginger bobbing up and down like a yo-yo outside his window, instantly spotted a potential customer and poked his nose out of the shop door. 'Are these kids bothering you, madam?' he asked in a smarmy voice.

'It's this poor little boy,' she said. 'I think he's fainted.'

'Is that all?' Mr Cumpsty said.

'You might show a little more concern,' the woman said, tartly.

'Not if you know him as well as I do! Nearly demolished my shop on more than one occasion, he has,' Mr Cumpsty said glumly. 'What are you two up to now, eh?'

'Nothing, honest,' Clyde said nervously.

But the woman wasn't to be put off. 'This poor boy could be seriously ill. Perhaps we ought to call an ambulance.'

'Yes, madam,' Mr Cumpsty said sarcastically. 'I wouldn't wonder if that's exactly what they're up to. That one,' he said, pointing at Ginger, 'would do anything for a free ride in an ambulance!'

'No, he wouldn't!' Clyde said quickly, alarm bells ringing in his head. He'd no idea what would happen if Ginger pressed the return button while his body was on its way to hospital. 'I'm sure he'll be all right in a minute.'

'Well, I'm not,' the woman said.

But as she spoke, Ginger began to stir. He came round so quickly and was so eager to tell Clyde about his latest journey that he didn't notice either of the grown-ups. 'What did I tell you?' he cried out. 'That is how it works.'

'And what did I tell you?' Mr Cumpsty said to the woman with a weary shake of his head.

'They thought you'd fainted,' Clyde explained. 'This lady wanted to call an ambulance.'

'And I,' Mr Cumpsty said sourly, 'wanted to send for the police!'

'I'm fine now, honest,' Ginger said.

'Does this happen to you very often?' the woman asked.

'Not until today!' Clyde murmured.

Ginger dug his elbow into Clyde's ribs. 'No!'

'If it happens again,' she insisted, 'I think you ought to see a doctor.'

'Or a psychiatrist!' Mr Cumpsty muttered angrily as

he stamped back into the shop.

'I'll be all right now, thanks,' Ginger promised the woman. He could hardly wait until she was out of earshot. 'You were dead right about the time thing, Clyde. I did go back to 1917, just like you said. When I popped into the shop to check, there was a new calendar hanging up with the year printed on it.'

'Okay, but next time you zoom off,' Clyde added, 'could you do it somewhere a bit less public? I mean, we've no idea what would have happened to you if they had carted your body off to hospital.'

Ginger shuddered at the frightening possibility of being permanently lost in time and space.

'Yes,' Ginger agreed, 'I guess you're right. I'd love to know how the watch really works. So far, judging by the dates marked off on the shop calendar, it's always taken me back to exactly the same date and time of day, only in different years. I wonder what would happen if I altered the date on the watch?'

'My dad always says about something new, "read the instructions only if desperate". In this case that could be a bit dodgy!'

But Ginger was lost in a fantasy of possibilities. 'Just think, maybe I could go back through all my birthdays and Christmases and open my presents all over again.'

'But you wouldn't get many surprises,' Clyde pointed out.

'No, but I once had a fantastic train set and there was this smashing BMX I got when I was seven. I wouldn't mind another go on that.'

'Hey, hang on,' Clyde suddenly said. 'Do you stay the same age when you travel back?'

'Course I do, stupid! I wasn't even born in 1917, was I?'

'So, if you went back to your seventh birthday you'd be too big for the bike, wouldn't you?'

'True,' Ginger agreed. Then another thought struck him. 'If I went back to my seventh birthday, do you think there'd be two of me – one aged seven and one like I am now?'

'One of you's plenty!' Clyde grinned, dodging the blow Ginger aimed at him. But something else had just occurred to Clyde. 'You went back to the same place as before, the shop and everything?' Ginger nodded. 'I expect that's because you were here when you pressed the button. I mean, if you were at the station, or at school, when you pressed the button, then you'd go back in time there instead.'

Ginger shook his head. 'I suppose, but there are so many things to try. If one of these other dials sets latitude and longitude, I could go anywhere in the world and it says it's waterproof.' Ginger pressed a combination of buttons so that new figures flashed up. 'I think this one's depth and this other must be height above sea level.'

'That could be really useful,' Clyde laughed. 'Suppose you set it so that you go back and suddenly appeared floating thirty feet above the ground!'

'I'd like to try that,' Ginger said poking about amongst the various controls.

'Hey, hang on, take it easy! If you get something wrong you could be stuck for ever amongst a bunch of dinosaurs.' Clyde stopped. 'Hey, what time is it now?'

'1945. That's during the Second World War!'

But Clyde had other things on his mind. 'Quarter to eight? Oh, no, I'm dead! I've just remembered, I promised Mum I'd be home at seven to look after our kid while she goes out. If I'm not back soon I'll be grounded. See you tomorrow and don't do anything daft!' And with that Clyde scooted off as fast as his legs would take him.

As Ginger made his way home he thought, 'I should have lent him the watch. Then he could easily have got back on time, or even before he left!'

'And where've you been 'til now?' Mum demanded the moment Ginger set foot in the kitchen.

'If only you knew!' Ginger thought to himself but decided to keep quiet. After all, they'd no sooner found out about Cass than they were forcing Ginger to give him back!

But nobody was listening.

'Gran's arrived,' Dad said.

Ginger loved Gran, but just at the moment his mind was far more on the mind-bending idea of being able to travel back and forth in time. 'Hello, Gran,' he said, giving her a peck on the cheek.

She returned the peck saying, 'Hello, Ronald.'

Ginger smiled patiently. 'I'm Ginger, Gran, not Ronald.'

Gran was ninety and apt to get very confused. She never knew what day of the week it was and her mind wandered freely between the present and her childhood. Several times she'd told Ginger she was late for school.

Ever since Grandad died Gran had lived with them.

When they'd moved to the shop, they were too busy to keep a close eye on her. She sometimes wandered off so, for her own safety, she'd agreed to move into an old folks' home where she could be looked after properly.

She *always* stayed with them for Christmas. And she enjoyed her other frequent visits, especially as she knew the area. She'd once lived in Mafeking Street.

'Well, we've all eaten,' Mum said. 'Yours is in the oven, probably all dried out by now.'

'What is it?' Ginger asked.

'Roast chicken.'

'Oh, I love chicken,' Gran piped, licking her lips.

'I know it's your favourite, Gran, that's why I got it,' Mum said.

'So, when are we eating?' Gran asked eagerly.

'You've just had yours, love,' Mum said gently.

'Oh!' Gran said.

She looked so disappointed Ginger suggested, 'You can have mine if you like.'

'Not for me, dear, thank you. I'm so full I couldn't eat another thing.'

After he'd eaten, Ginger was about to settle down with the rest of the family in front of the television when his mother suddenly asked the dreaded question, 'Ginger, haven't you got any homework to do?'

Reluctantly, Ginger went up to his bedroom. He had to write an essay for Miss Moss with the dreary title 'My Most Exciting Journey'. 'And remember,' she'd said, 'this should be a factual account, but I want plenty of lively description, so that I can imagine I'm accompanying you on the journey.'

Ginger's problem was, until today, he'd never been

on an exciting journey in his life but he could hardly write about travelling back to the beginning of the century because nobody, apart from Clyde, would ever believe it had happened.

Clyde was going to write about his parents taking him to meet his grandparents in Jamaica. One of the girls intended to write about leaving the village in India where she was born and crossing the Arabian Sea in a freighter on the first part of her journey to Britain. Most of the others, unlike Ginger, had at least been abroad. Ginger's trip on the train to Scarborough seemed neither exciting nor memorable.

Suddenly Ginger thought of using his watch to check his memory of the journey against the reality. So he went down to ask his parents the date of their trip but they couldn't agree about the year, let alone a date.

'It was the year Janice had chicken pox,' Mum said.

'Not if it was when I was ten,' Janice cut in. 'That was the summer I had German measles.'

'No, love,' Mum shook her head. 'That was mumps and it was the year before.'

'As a little girl, I had mumps very badly,' Gran added.

At that point, beginning to wonder if they'd ever really been to Scarborough, Ginger left them comparing illnesses, went back upstairs and relied on his own memory.

When Ginger fell asleep, the watch was still firmly strapped to his wrist and his mind was racing through all the amazing things he'd like to try with it. But in the middle of the night Ginger suddenly became aware of somebody violently shaking him, shining a torch directly into his eyes and shouting, 'Wake up! Wake up!'

For a terrifying moment Ginger wondered if, in his sleep, he'd been fiddling with his watch and he had got transported back to the Second World War only to be interrogated by the Gestapo.

But it was Gran, her thin grey hair neatly plaited, wearing a dressing gown over her nightdress, standing beside his bed. 'What's up, Gran?' Ginger asked drowsily.

'Time to get up, or you'll be late for work. Your breakfast's all ready in the kitchen.'

Ginger glanced at his watch and sighed. 'Gran, it's two o'clock in the morning, I don't have to get up for hours yet!'

Gran blinked and looked a little puzzled, but she didn't argue and allowed Ginger to lead her back to her room, where he settled her back into bed.

'Good night, Gran,' he said as he switched off the light.

'Good night, Jack,' she called after him.

Why does everyone keep calling me Jack? Ginger wondered as he popped down to the kitchen to check that Gran hadn't left anything on the cooker.

Dad wouldn't be pleased if they had another fire so soon after the one the crooks had started. Gran had a habit of leaving empty kettles boiling, or she forgot she was cooking vegetables. Usually the only warning was a dreadful smell of burning from the dried-out, blackened pan.

As Ginger gratefully wolfed down the porridge Gran

had made, he couldn't help thinking in a way how lucky she was. 'Gran doesn't need a watch to travel around in time – she does it all by herself!'

17

Time for a change

Maybe it was because Ginger had a disturbed night, but he overslept the following morning. He was late getting up for his paper round and late returning for breakfast.

'You're going to have to rush,' Mum warned, hastily buttering him a round of toast.

'Where's Gran?'

'She's worrying about her Great Sorrow again.'

Gran's Great Sorrow, as the family called it, was from some incident in her dim and distant past, though Ginger didn't know if it was real or imaginary. But it was so real to Gran that sometimes she would rock back and forth in her chair for hours, moaning, talking agitatedly to herself and sometimes bursting into floods of tears.

'She's probably tired from last night,' Mum explained, 'so I persuaded her to have breakfast in bed.'

'Great!' Ginger gasped. 'I'm tired too, but nobody suggested I should have breakfast in bed!'

'It's different for you,' Mum said airily. 'You're young, with bags of energy, you'll recover more easily. Besides you've got to go to school. And it's a quarter to nine and you won't make it if you don't leave *now*!'

Ginger was almost out of the door as she called after him, 'Sure you've got everything?'

'Yes, Mum,' he shouted back.

But he'd hardly sat at his desk in Miss Moss's English class when he remembered, his homework was still at home in his bedroom.

Ginger wasn't alone. A couple of people near the front had forgotten theirs too and Miss Moss's temper was getting worse as she worked her way towards Ginger.

She was a short, dumpy woman who wore long shapeless skirts. Her bush of dark, wiry hair, which was always decorated with a collection of raggedy bows and clips and often skewered by her red-rimmed glasses, was about as tidy as an explosion in a wire works.

Normally a quiet person, if crossed she turned into a gorilla running amuck. By the time she'd reached the middle of the room and six people had failed to hand in work, she was ready to go into orbit. 'I just hope the rest of you have remembered, otherwise detentions are going to be showering down on you like snow!'

Ginger decided this was no time for fine detail. He swiftly re-set his watch back to half-past eight, half an hour before school started. A split second before he pressed the gold button, he hissed across to Clyde, 'Cover for me!' and then he was gone.

Because there was so little difference in the times, the blackness he experienced was so short the people around him almost seemed to fade away until Ginger found himself sitting alone in a deserted classroom.

'Right, now all I have to do is to run back home,

collect my homework and hope it'll travel back through time with me in my pocket.'

But when he tried to leave he quickly learned that it wasn't going to be quite that easy. The classroom door was locked as they always were in between classes.

And when he crossed to the window, there was Herman Munster, the school's Neanderthal caretaker, his knuckles trailing along the tarmac yard as he searched obsessively for litter. Everyone reckoned he ate it all, Coke cans, the lot! Which explained why, when he belched, it sounded like metal cogs grinding together.

'Now I'm really stuck!'

Ginger looked round for another method of escape and noticed the ventilator window above the door. Though it was as broad as the door, the V-shaped gap which opened on to the corridor was tiny. 'But I might just be able to wriggle through it. The real problem is getting up there.'

Ginger dragged a desk across to the door but, when he stood on it, although he could reach the window, he wasn't yet high enough to be able to climb through. He perched a chair on the desk, but even that wasn't quite enough. Finally he added a pile of books.

He scrambled up his rickety, makeshift ladder, heaved himself up by gripping the frame and managed to get his head through the opening.

Two things happened at once.

First, his feet sent the books and chair flying across the classroom to land with a crash which echoed through the empty school.

Secondly, Ginger discovered he was stuck, halfway

through the ventilator; feet in the air, hanging head down into the corridor like a freeze-framed diver.

Herman, attracted by the racket was banging his fists against the classroom window. 'Nutt! You've no right to be in there!' Ginger, not for the first time, cursed his hair which was always a dead giveaway. 'I'll report you to the Headmaster for this, Nutt!'

Ginger gave one final, enormous wriggle, and plunged, head-first, on to the tiled floor. Dazed, but anxious to avoid Herman's clutches, he picked himself up and hared off down the corridor, out of the back door. He was over the wall halfway home before Herman reached the corner of the building.

Breathless, Ginger glanced at his watch. Twenty to nine. He was just in time.

Dad didn't seem at all surprised to see him. 'Mum's got your breakfast waiting.'

This time, before he went into the kitchen, Ginger raced upstairs and collected the essay which he stuffed into his trouser pocket.

His mother was busy buttering a round of toast. 'Great!' thought Ginger. 'This way I even get two breakfasts!'

'You're going to have to rush,' she said, just as she had before.

'Where's Gran?' he asked.

'She's worrying about her Great Sorrow again . . .'

As Mum prattled on, repeating the conversation, Ginger couldn't help wondering what would happen if he changed something, asked a totally different question?

Ginger decided as he was there it would be fun to

find out, so he suddenly said, 'I'm not sure I ought to tell you this, Mum. You know I hate telling tales, but when I walked past Janice's room I'm sure I could smell cigarette smoke.'

'What?'

'It was only a faint whiff, maybe I dreamt it. Do you want me to go and check?' he asked innocently.

'Don't bother, I'll check on Janice!' Mum said grimly, before slipping back into the original conversation. 'Besides you've got to go to school. And it's a quarter to nine and you won't make it if you don't leave *now*!'

But when he ran into the school yard with the last bell already ringing, Ginger knew he had to be sitting at his desk before he could press the button but Herman was waiting to pounce.

Clyde once told Ginger, after Herman had jumped on him for dropping a sweet wrapper, 'It's like having a house fall on you!'

'Nutt! Come here, I want you,' Herman roared.

'Can't stop now, Mr Munsey, I'm late for class.'

Ginger dodged round Herman's outstretched paws and raced into school just in time to find Miss Moss, surrounded by the rest of the class, struggling with the classroom door.

'There's a desk jammed behind it, Miss,' Ginger suggested helpfully.

'Don't be silly, Nutt,' Miss Moss said scornfully. 'How could there be?'

'I bet if two of us pushed really hard, it'd open,' Ginger said.

'I doubt it,' Miss Moss said, 'but you may try if you wish.'

Ginger and Clyde together heaved and very slowly, with a loud squeal of protest from inside as the desk skidded across the polished floor, they slowly forced the door open far enough for them to squeeze through. 'It *was* a desk, Miss.'

Miss Moss looked slightly suspicious. 'How on earth did you know that, Nutt?'

'Oh, that's nothing, Miss,' Ginger boasted. 'Everyone knows I'm a psychic!'

'Psycho more like,' Debbie Catling suggested.

But Miss Moss wasn't listening. 'I still don't understand how that desk was placed behind the door when it was locked from the outside.'

'Somebody climbed over, Miss,' Mugsy suggested.

'Yes, Miss,' Debbie said. 'Like they do when they climb over the dividing walls in the girls' toilets and lock all the doors from the inside, so nobody can get in!'

'Been caught short, Debbie?' Mugsy laughed.

'That's enough,' Miss Moss said. 'Seats, everyone, we're late as it is.'

They'd hardly found their places when Miss Moss began to collect the homework. As she reached the middle of the room and again made her threatening announcement about detentions showering down like snow, Ginger panicked.

Until that moment he'd always intended to press the button before Miss Moss reached him, but his courage failed. He wasn't convinced that the essay, which he'd gone to so much trouble to collect, would travel forwards with him.

True, the money had gone back to 1913, but it *had* changed in the process and so had his clothes.

On the other hand, if he handed the essay in now, would Miss Moss still have it after he'd pressed the magic button?

Every second brought her closer but he still couldn't make up his mind what to do for the best.

The classroom door burst open and a little first year poked her head in.

Miss Moss turned and glared at her. 'Yes, what is it?'

The girl blushed and silently waved a note in the air.

'I'm sorry,' Miss Moss boomed, 'I was never a Girl Guide, I don't read semaphore.'

The class laughed dutifully, but the poor girl looked about to burst into tears, so Miss Moss relented. 'If it's a note, please just give it to me.'

The girl scooted down between the desks, stuffed the note into Miss Moss's hand and fled, followed by a roar of laughter.

'That's enough,' Miss Moss said as she read the note and then announced, 'Nutt, the Head wants to see you at first break.'

Ginger instantly decided that things were getting too hairy in the past and he firmly pressed the button. He experienced a brief blackout, so brief that he wasn't sure if the watch had done its stuff properly.

Miss Moss said, 'Nutt! Were you asleep?'

'No, miss,' he said, sighing with relief because if she thought he *had* been asleep then he must really have got back.

She looked at his empty desk. 'And where's your homework?'

Anxiously Ginger stuffed his hand in his pocket and discovered, with enormous relief, that the paper was still there!

Miss Moss made a big thing of unfolding the grubby, creased, sheet of paper and held it up in the air by two fingers as if she'd found a dirty tissue. 'I suppose it's better than nothing,' she said, 'but only just! Don't forget the Head wants to see you.'

Ginger was shocked. The moment he'd pushed the button he'd honestly expected to leave all the business with Herman behind him. Then, as Miss Moss made her way back to the front of the class, Ginger also noticed the desk was still standing just behind the door!

18

Time warped!

During break Ginger had a very sticky conversation with Nobby Dore, the Head while Herman leered at him from the corner.

'Mr Munsey here is positive he saw you in the classroom before the school bell had rung. What bothers me most is, if all the doors were locked and the outside windows shut, how on earth did you get in there in the first place?'

Ginger swiftly picked that point up and worried it like a dog. 'That's the whole point, sir. It's impossible, isn't it? I couldn't have been, could I? I mean, I'm not Paul Daniels.'

Nobby shut him up with a piercing stare. 'But Munsey saw you, Nutt.' A darker cloud suddenly passed over Nobby's round, pink face. 'You didn't get yourself locked in on purpose and spend the night in there for some sort of silly bet, did you? You might as well own up, Nutt, it'll only make things easier in the long run.'

But Ginger had been caught like that before, pleading guilty to what sounded like a lesser charge, only to suffer the original punishment and more besides. 'No, sir.'

'Well, let's leave that issue aside for a moment. The fact remains that Munsey saw you in there, you can't deny that.'

'What time was this, sir?'

Nobby turned to Herman who without hesitation said, 'Half-past eight, Mr Dore. I can be certain, because at the time I was on patrol in the yard . . .'

'Yes, yes, Munsey!' Nobby said testily, wishing that Munsey would forget he'd spent ten years as a private in the Catering Corps.

'Well, that's it then!' Ginger said triumphantly. 'If it was half-past eight, it couldn't possibly have been me, sir. I overslept this morning. I was at home with me mum having breakfast until quarter to nine. In fact, don't you remember, Herma . . . I mean, Mr Munsey, when I met you at the gate this morning the last bell was ringing.'

'Yes, so?'

But Nobby could see what Ginger was getting at even if Herman couldn't. 'You say you saw him, Munsey?'

'Oh, yes, Mr Dore,' Herman said proudly. 'I attempted to apprehend him on entry to the premises, but he evaded capture.'

Nobby's irritation was now focused solely on Herman. 'I think we'll leave it there, Mr Munsey! You've obviously got your facts muddled.'

But Herman wasn't used to being proved wrong. 'You must have run out and come back in again,' he floundered.

'Run out of a locked classroom?' Ginger asked quietly.

'I mean, climbed out. That was what you were doing when I spotted you.'

Nobby's patience was exhausted. 'Really, Munsey! One minute you say you saw him running and the next he's climbing.'

Ginger enjoyed watching Herman squirm and couldn't resist adding, 'Seeing things can be a very serious problem, I'd see a doctor about that.'

'Don't push your luck, Nutt!' Nobby snapped. 'You're not off the hook until I get a note from your mother which backs up your story. Out!'

As Ginger shut Nobby's door he grinned when he heard Nobby laying into Herman, 'Next time, before you come in here accusing people, get your facts straight, Munsey!'

Over lunch, a very confused Ginger said to Clyde, 'The thing that bothers me is that desk.'

Clyde looked blank. 'What desk?'

'The one behind the door in English.'

'What's odd about that?' Clyde asked. 'We shifted it together before class.'

'You really remember doing that?'

'Of course I do,' Clyde said.

'But I put that desk there when I went back in time, so that I could climb out. I didn't expect it to be there when I returned. But Herman still remembers seeing me in the classroom and you know about shifting the desk.'

Clyde couldn't understand what Ginger was getting at. 'Of course I do! I was there when it happened, wasn't I?'

'No, you weren't, that's the whole point!' Ginger said. 'That only happened when I went back. This morning, when we first went into the classroom there was nothing blocking the door.'

'You're off your trolley!' Clyde scoffed.

'Clyde,' Ginger insisted, 'I'll swear to it on a stack of Adrian Mole's diaries!'

'But in that case,' Clyde said doubtfully, 'how is it Miss Moss, Herman and me, all know what happened?'

'I don't know *how*,' Ginger said. 'But you realise what it means?' Clyde shook his head. 'It means that when you travel back through time you can alter history.'

'Oh, yes!' Clyde said scornfully. 'So why don't you zoom back to 1938 and shoot Hitler? That'd wipe out the Second World War. Or go back to last Saturday's football match and save the goal you let in, so we'd still be top of the table?'

'You're cracked!'

'I'm cracked? You're the one who says it can be done,' Clyde said, poking Ginger in the chest.

Ginger knocked Clyde's hand away. 'Talk sense! I couldn't do either of those things. For a start I'd have to be in Berlin, or somewhere, to get anywhere near Hitler and I'd probably stand no more chance of saving that goal this time than I did before,' he admitted. 'But I'll find some way of proving it to you, don't you worry.'

'Well, you've got a real chance next period,' Clyde grinned, 'we've got history!'

Yes, thought Ginger, that'd be perfect!

All through history, while Mr Lodge rabbited on about the week-long siege during the Civil War which took place in the derelict church where Ginger and Clyde's tree house was, Ginger racked his brains to find a way of proving to Clyde that what he'd said about changing events was true.

The trouble is, Ginger silently admitted to himself, if I come back after I've done something and nobody can remember the previous version, there isn't much point. It's a bit like recording over a film you've got on video – nobody can see what used to be there.

Mr Lodge droned on. 'And the siege ended in disaster on 4 August 1644, all through the thoughtless actions of one silly little boy, Jethro. If Jethro had only stayed put, the Royalists might have survived but, probably because he was a bit on the greedy side and there was not enough food, Jethro sneaked out through a back window and tried to escape. But the Roundheads saw him, killed him and, thinking he was the start of a mass escape, set fire to the church and the hundred other people, mainly women and children who were locked in there, all died. Simply because of one stupid boy!'

Ginger piped up, 'How do you know all that, sir?'

Mr Lodge looked surprised by Ginger's unusual interest. 'Contemporary records of course, boy.'

'But all the Royalists were killed, sir,' Ginger pointed out. 'So the stories would be a bit one-sided? The Roundheads doing a whitewash job as an excuse for wiping out the Royalists.'

'There was one other source of information,' Mr Lodge said, 'but not a very reliable one, I'm afraid. A boy called Seth, who had been away on an errand, returned to the village after the Roundheads had besieged the church. Not knowing what else to do, he hid so that he could see what was going on. Long afterwards, Seth wrote an account which tried to show Jethro was a hero rather than a villain.'

'Why don't you believe him, sir?'

'Two reasons, Nutt. First: Jethro and Seth were very good friends and as we all know, friends often stick together, even if that means lying to protect each other! Second: the account wasn't written at the time of the siege but years later, after the monarchy had been restored, and we all know that distance lends enchantment.'

Ginger didn't. 'What does that mean?'

'It means, for instance,' said Mr Lodge, with an evil gleam in his eye, 'that long after I've retired, I shall probably remember you, Nutt, as a harmless case, rather than the grubby, impudent and uneducated boy I currently describe in your annual report.'

Mr Lodge paused and preened himself during the laughter he'd provoked.

'And now, Nutt, with your permission, we'll get on. Next Thursday we shall be, against my better judgement, going on a site visit to the ruined church.' He glared as a delighted murmur rippled round the room. 'This is not an excuse for a picnic. You're going to work and I have prepared sheets which you will fill in on site!'

Loud groans.

'However, before we go, for homework I want you to write, as if you'd been a reporter at the scene, a newspaper account of the siege. But remember, this is for a seventeenth-century newspaper, not the *Sun*!' he said, deliberately aiming the remark at Ginger. 'So I'd be grateful if you would stick to facts rather than bothering with idle speculation. That's what history is about, Nutt, facts!'

But Ginger, still smarting from Mr Lodge's attack, was only half-listening. He was too busy working out a plan which, by using his watch, might prove his smug teacher wrong.

19

A whiff of the past

Ginger's last doubt about being able to change the past disappeared the moment he arrived home from school. He was met by a very angry Janice. She grabbed hold of his ear. 'Come here, you little worm!'

'Hey! Get off! That hurts!' Ginger protested.

'If I had my way,' Janice said, twisting his ear between her thumb and forefinger, 'I'd pull you apart and stuff the bits in the liquidiser.'

'What's up with you?'

'Why did you tell Mum I'd been smoking?'

'Can't you take a joke?' Ginger tried to laugh, which wasn't easy while his reddening ear was being twisted into the shape of a snail shell.

'Joke? You nearly got me grounded for a month.'

'Sorry,' Ginger said, struggling hard to sound as if he meant it.

'Sorry's not enough. I'm going to make you pay this time, Ginger.'

'Anything!' Ginger squealed.

'Something so awful, you'll never do anything bad to me again.' Janice almost dribbled at the prospect.

'Just let go of my ear before you rip it off.' Janice freed him and he cupped his injured ear in his hand.

'So what is it you want me to do?'

'I haven't decided yet. I'll decide by the time you get back from delivering your papers.'

As she pranced off up the stairs Ginger called after her, 'Don't kiss any princes, in case they turn into toads!'

'Right!' Janice shouted as she raced down. 'This time you die!'

Ginger was narrowly rescued from total demolition by Gran coming out of the kitchen bound for the sitting room. She hadn't heard the argument but, with one of her rare flashes of total understanding, she sensed the searing heat being exchanged between her grandchildren. As she passed between them she smiled sweetly and brought out one of her old-fashioned sayings, 'Little birds in their nests should agree.'

Ginger and Janice were left pulling grotesque smiles at each other, but the second Gran closed the sitting-room door, Ginger fired his final shot. 'Not if one of them's a great fat cuckoo!'

Then he bolted to the safety of a shop full of customers before Janice could grab him again.

But while he was out delivering papers he was aware that Janice would be waiting for him when he returned and he racked his brains for some way he could fix her for good. The answer came as he was delivering a paper to a house with a disgustingly smelly dustbin.

'That's it! And it'll give me a chance to try re-setting my watch before I risk going to the Civil War!'

On his way home, Ginger carefully set his watch back a year and pressed the magic button before popping into the open-all-hours mini-mart. Getting back into the house without anyone spotting him wasn't a problem. Dad was serving in the shop, Janice was gawping at her favourite TV soap and Mum was in the kitchen cooking tea.

Ginger crept upstairs to the landing. Janice had recently taken to locking her door but, being in the past, that was no longer a problem. As he opened the door and entered the Chamber of Horrors, the macabre jumble sale, all decorated in black which Janice called her room, Ginger muttered, 'Maybe, to ward off the evil spirits in here, I should have bought some garlic too!'

However, he tugged out the package he had bought, slit the plastic covering with Janice's nail scissors and slid the whole thing under some of the few garments which must have accidentally found their way on to her wardrobe shelf.

Out on the landing, Ginger heard Janice galumphing up the stairs. Although he'd never before risked going back to a different physical place when returning through time, he had no desire to be caught, at any time, coming out of Janice's room. Ginger hastily pressed the button and was whirled forwards through time.

As he came round, Ginger was aware of somebody standing over him. It was Janice, but far from being angry, she seemed concerned.

'Mum!' she called out. 'Ginger's passed out on the landing!'

While he waited for Mum to arrive, Ginger moaned a little and clutched feebly at his stomach.

'Janice, what have you done to him now?'

'Nothing, honest! I just came up and found him lying here.'

Ginger opened his eyes and uttered the line he'd heard so often on the telly. 'What happened?'

'You must have fainted, love,' his mother said sympathetically.

'Perhaps I've been overdoing things,' he suggested hopefully. 'What with school, all that homework and my paper rounds.'

'I don't think so,' Mum smiled gently. 'Maybe you've caught a bit of a chill.'

'Should I have a day off school?' he offered eagerly.

'No,' his mother replied, noting the instant improvement, 'but, just to be on the safe side, maybe you should stay in and rest this weekend, instead of going off with Clyde.'

'Oh, I think I'll be okay now,' Ginger said hastily. Then he paused and sniffed dramatically. 'Hey, you remember that smell I mentioned this morning . . .'

'Ginger!' warned Janice.

'Don't start stirring up trouble again!' Mum said.

'But hang on,' Ginger protested. 'I thought it was smoke, but it isn't. It's something much worse. Can't you smell it, Mum?'

Mum sniffed and she pulled a face. 'Yes, I can now you mention it, it's awful.'

'Maybe that's what made me faint,' Ginger said and added for good measure, 'it seems to be coming from Janice's room.'

'Ginger!' Janice shrieked.

But Mum was in no mood for argument. 'Janice, unlock that door.'

Under protest, Janice did as she was told and suddenly a vast wave of some dreadful, overpowering smell swept over them.

'No wonder you fainted,' Mum said, her voice muffled by the hand she was using to cover her nose and mouth. 'Janice, what on earth have you got in here?'

'Nothing, Mum,' Janice wailed and she rounded on Ginger. 'Is this another of your tricks?'

'How could it be?' Ginger said innocently. 'Your room's always locked and none of us can get in there, because you've got the only key, remember?'

'I've asked you to clear this place up a thousand times,' Mum ranted on. 'There's piles of dirty clothes all over the place, half-eaten sandwiches and half a pot of yoghurt that's been here so long it's growing mould!'

'Smells gruesome to me,' Ginger said and dived downstairs to the sitting room, satisfied his amazing watch, the package from the mini-market and the ageing process caused by the time jump, had fixed Janice good and proper!

Gran had woken from her sleep. She was sitting with her old photograph album, something she never travelled without, open on her lap. But instead of looking at it, she was gazing unhappily into space.

'What's up, Gran?' Ginger asked.

She looked at him vaguely. 'Oh, hello, Jack. It's a while since I saw you.'

'I'm Ginger.'

She wasn't taking in anything. 'Are you still in the army?'

'No, Gran, I go to school.'

But she wasn't listening and Ginger saw her face crumple as she sighed, 'Oh, dear.'

'What's the matter, Gran?'

He rested his hand on hers and was astonished at how bony and cold she felt.

'Oh, the shame of it all!' she moaned.

'Of what, Gran?' Ginger asked, hoping that at last he might find out more about Gran's Great Sorrow than his parents had told him.

But before she could reply, Mum came storming into the room. 'Look what I found under a sweater in Janice's wardrobe.' She held up a plastic bag with some hideous festering substance lurking in the bottom.

'What on earth is it, Mum?' Ginger asked innocently.

'The rotting remains of a kipper, if you please. I can't think what possessed her. It's so far gone, you'd think it had been lying hidden up there for a year!'

Ginger smirked to himself!

20

Heroes and villains

Ginger took Clyde down to the old church, aiming to prove his theory about being able to change historical fact. But when they arrived, they were surprised to find a bright yellow pick-up truck parked by the gate and hear men's voices drifting across the usually deserted churchyard.

Using the rhododendrons for cover, they crept closer to find out what was going on. Three men in overalls were gathered around the huge old oak tree which grew in the far corner of the churchyard. They seemed to be discussing what to do about several large branches which had been snapped off and brought down by the recent high winds, blocking the footpath.

'Oh, well, that's knocked everything on the head!' Ginger hissed to Clyde.

'I don't see what difference them being here makes to you,' Clyde whispered back. 'You'll be gone and I'll be the one left to explain, for the umpteenth time, why you've passed out. But if you don't want anyone to see you,' Clyde suggested, 'why don't we climb up to the tree house before you press the button?'

'I could,' Ginger said, doubtfully, 'but don't you think I might catch somebody's attention if I land in

1644, fifteen feet above ground with no tree?!'

Clyde stuffed his fist in his mouth to avoid laughing out loud.

'Hey, shut up!' Ginger hissed. 'They're coming!'

The two boys ducked as the men, still discussing the tree, ambled towards them.

'Taking the broken branches off is easy enough,' one of them, a big man with a red face, said, 'but I reckon we'd be better off cutting the whole thing down. It'll only save us a job later on.'

'It's not as easy as that,' the man who seemed to be in charge said. 'That tree's at least four hundred years old, there's a protection order on it.'

'Aye, well, a protection order won't keep a rotten tree standing.'

'We'll still have to check at the office first,' the foreman said.

The third man spoke for the first time. 'I just hope it doesn't fall on somebody and kill them while the office are still making up their minds.'

And with that, all three headed for their van.

'Right,' Clyde said, 'now they've cleared off, let's get on with it before it gets too dark.'

'It's got to be dark, otherwise the sentries will be able to see me,' Ginger said.

'That's all very well for you,' Clyde grumbled, 'but I hate the idea of standing over your body in a churchyard at dead of night. Suppose somebody saw me? They'd probably think I'd murdered you and I might yet if you don't get on with it.'

'Okay! Don't rush me,' Ginger said. 'We've got to get in position yet. I know my clothes will change during the journey, but I won't know whether I'm going to arrive dressed as a Royalist or a Roundhead until I get there. I don't want to turn up bang in the middle of the wrong lines, do I? We must find a spot where the Puritan soldiers won't see me and yet I'll be able to see everything. Where's that diagram?'

Clyde unfolded a sheet of paper which showed the position of the Roundhead soldiers in relation to the church, which he'd copied down from the board during History. Pointing to one corner he said, 'I think you'll be safe enough by the gate. With the wall for cover, they'll have a hard job seeing you, but you could see them and still be able to watch the back of the church as well.'

'I'd better take that with me in case I need to check anything,' Ginger said, stuffing the map into the pocket of his jeans. He took a deep breath, carefully set the watch for the evening of 4 August 1644 and said, 'Okay, wish me luck, here I go.'

'Don't hang about there, will you?' Clyde said, but it was too late. Ginger was already lying stretched out alongside the church wall. Clyde shivered uneasily in the gathering gloom.

As Ginger hurtled through the darkness he thought the whirling and turning would never end. He was ready for the idea that it would take longer than simply going back to the early part of his own century, but had never realised it would take so long, or be so cold!

From what he'd read about spaceships returning or leaving earth, he knew things which travelled fast got hotter. What he'd overlooked was that in time travel there was no atmosphere to create that kind of friction.

The further back in time he went, the more it felt like sledging down a hill at night. Flecks of ice caught his half-closed eyes and scratched his face and hands. The icy blast gnawed through to the very marrow of his bones.

All this just to prove old Lodge wrong, Ginger thought, I must be out of my head.

Twice, during this eternity, Ginger was more than ready to give up. But, although he managed to press the gold button and braced himself for the shock of being thrown into reverse, nothing happened. Worse, it seemed to act as an accelerator, hurling him forwards even faster and more violently than before, until he blacked out completely. He came to, a mass of bruises, his skin feeling as if he'd been dragged along a gravel path.

Slowly Ginger became aware of distant voices and an unpleasant smell. Cautiously he struggled up and peered across the right angle of the churchyard wall.

Away to his left, roughly where it was marked on Clyde's diagram, Ginger could see the Roundheads' camp fires dully lighting the makeshift shelters they'd built.

'I'm glad Mr Lodge got that right!' he muttered thankfully.

Though when he looked down to check his clothes, he realised it would hardly have mattered where he'd landed. He wore a drab, coarse shirt, the sleeves of which ended at the elbow, leaving the watch on his wrist looking odd and very exposed. His dark trousers ended at the shins in thick cuffs and though he had a stiff, unyielding pair of leather boots, his legs and feet were otherwise bare.

The outfit offered little protection against the intense cold of the night and he wasn't pleased to discover that some of the smell of cheesy football socks was coming from him, as if neither he, nor his clothes had been washed in months. But fouler smells drifted across from the soldiers' insanitary camp following a week of laying siege to the church.

From time to time lumps of thick black cloud, driven by a strong wind, suddenly blotted out the full moon, making its cold, staring eye blink. Bored sentries, keeping half an eye on the church, leant against their muskets. Beside them, wooden stakes, driven into the ground, held smoking flares, bathing the churchyard in a flickering, dismal light.

The untidy undergrowth and fir trees, including the one containing their tree house, had disappeared, though Ginger could make out the outlines of a couple of yew trees and a younger, smaller version of the oak. Apart from these, only the occasional outlines of a few ghostly, white tombs cast any shadows on the expanse of short uneven grass which lay between the wall and the church.

Expecting to see the church fully restored to its former glory, Ginger was surprised to find it much smaller, minus all its Victorian additions. There was no tower. Only a long, low stone building with a pitched slate roof. Towards one end of the side wall was a heavy, wooden door, deeply gashed and splintered as if someone had tried to batter it down.

Its narrow windows had no glass and although some were covered with cloth, others were open and through these Ginger caught the occasional low murmur of voices and the more persistent cry of a baby. As people inside moved, the feeble light from a few guttering tallow candles cast huge, eerie shadows.

Suddenly a louder noise came from one of the front windows facing the Roundheads' camp. An argument had broken out and Ginger distinctly heard a boy shout, 'Let go of me! I'll wait no longer. I'm not frightened of them!'

Though the sentries stirred, they'd been idle too long to expect anything dramatic and so none was ready for the tousled, blond head of a boy which appeared in one of the windows.

Swiftly the boy kicked off hands inside the church which struggled to pull him back. He fell from the window, scrambled up and ran across past the door towards the oak.

'Halt!' shouted one of the sentries, grabbing his musket. The others, alerted by his call, also raised theirs.

In his plans for this expedition, Ginger had always seen himself as the hero who would change the course of history and save the boy, if indeed this really was Jethro. Ginger would leap over the wall to draw the sentries' fire, so that Jethro could escape in the confusion. But faced with the reality of loaded muskets, Ginger froze. Until that moment he'd never seriously considered the possibility of being shot.

If he were wounded he might never be able to press the watch and return to his own world and if he were killed in 1644, surely he couldn't still be alive in the twentieth century?

In the seconds it took for that thought to flash through Ginger's brain the boy had reached the trunk of the oak tree. He turned defiantly to face the soldiers and called out, in a thin, high voice, 'I have no fear of you, I am for the King and I'm going for help!'

'Run, you idiot, run!' Ginger shouted as loud as he could, but his voice was drowned by the sharp cracks from the sentries' muskets and Ginger watched in horror as the boy's body jerked and twitched, peppered with shot, before he collapsed on the ground.

The sickly Fireworks Night smell of burnt gunpowder drifted across the eerily-silent churchyard.

A woman screamed inside the church and, although Ginger knew it was useless, he was about to scramble over the churchyard wall when a strong pair of hands shot out of the dark, grabbed hold of him and threw him to the ground. Though it was impossible to see more than the outline of his attacker, Ginger felt the dull weight of a body sitting astride his stomach, pinning him down.

A metal blade flashed briefly before an earthy hand was clamped over his face and there was the smell of foul breath, as his attacker hissed into his ear, 'Make another move or sound and I'll slit you open from gullet to guts!'

21

A matter of life and death

'You're a spy! A Puritan spy,' declared Ginger's assailant.

'No, I'm not,' Ginger spluttered. 'You're Seth, aren't you?'

'If you're no spy, how come you know my name?' Seth thrust the knife up close, until Ginger felt the sharp point prick his neck.

'All right,' Ginger agreed. 'I'm not going to do anything, I promise.'

'You'd best not,' Seth warned, removing the hand that covered Ginger's eyes.

As he looked up in the half-light, Ginger caught a glimpse of a boy of about his own age, with cropped black hair, wearing clothes similar to his own. The broad blade of the vicious-looking knife and the determined expression in the boy's dark eyes, convinced Ginger that Seth meant business.

'Empty your pockets,' Seth instructed. 'Slow and easy.'

There was little to show. A few coins, some pieces of string and Clyde's diagram.

Seth snatched up the paper, which had changed into coarser and flimsier material and peered at the drawing. It now appeared to have been done in black ink rather than with Clyde's blue ballpoint. 'What's this?'

'A map of the Roundheads' camp.'

'And, if you're no spy, why are you carrying this?'

Ginger quickly dismissed the idea to try to explain he'd brought the plan with him from the twentieth century. He'd had enough trouble convincing Clyde – there was no way he could explain something so unlikely to a nervous, frightened boy. Particularly one holding a lethal-looking knife.

Ginger's brain raced as he struggled to invent a more likely explanation. 'I was going to run and get help to save the people in the church.'

'But I don't know you, you're not from around these parts.'

'I am, sort of,' Ginger stumbled, adding hastily, 'I've got relatives here.'

'Oh? Who?' Seth asked suspiciously.

This was getting too complicated for Ginger! 'There's no time to waste. I've got to take this plan to our troops so they can take the enemy by surprise and rescue the people in the church before they're burned to death.'

'Burned to death!' Seth scoffed. 'Mad the Roundheads may be, but they'd never dare do anything so evil!'

'I know they will,' Ginger insisted, 'if we don't stop them.'

Seth's eyes narrowed. 'And how could you *know* such a thing if you're not on their side?'

'Let's just say it's a gift, I can see into the future.'

'You're a witch's son?'

'No, of course not.'

'For if you are, you'll be the one who burns!'

'There's no time to lose,' Ginger tried to impress upon Seth. 'If I don't go and get help now, it'll be too late.'

Ginger struggled to escape, but Seth pushed him down again, thrusting the knife towards Ginger's stomach with one hand, whilst catching hold of a handful of shirt with the other. 'You'll go nowhere until I say! There are too many things about you which don't make sense.' His eyes lit on Ginger's watch and he grabbed the wrist. 'What's this – some machine of the Devil?'

'It's a watch,' Ginger said, frantically trying to pull his arm free of Seth's iron grip.

'I've seen no timepiece like that before. Besides, by the look of you, you could never afford such a grand thing, so how come it fell into your hands?'

'It was a present,' Ginger said, still struggling without success.

'Oh, yes?' Seth sneered. 'Then you can give it to me now. For if you're not in league with the Devil, I'm beginning to think you're nothing but a common criminal. A looter who profits from others' misfortunes. So what's not yours by right, can just as easily be mine. Hand it over!'

Ginger knew that without the watch he might as well be dead. He would risk everything to keep it. 'No, I won't,' he said defiantly.

'Then I'll have to take it, won't I?'

Seth was about to cut through the strap, when loud

voices in the churchyard distracted his attention. As he knelt up to peer over the wall, Ginger joined him.

The sentries had been joined by other soldiers from the camp and one man, taller than the others, was shouting orders to his troops. 'Bring hay and straw from the horse lines,' he cried.

'Who's that?' Ginger whispered.

'Colonel Praise-God Jones,' Seth said, spitting on the ground to demonstrate his hatred. 'He was the one who ordered this siege, but there's nobody in the church except harmless women, children and men too old to leave and fight for the King. They took shelter when they learned that Cromwell's men were coming. I would have gone to fight with the other men if I'd been here.'

Ginger could easily believe that Seth was bloodthirsty enough to make a formidable soldier. 'Why didn't you?'

'My father's a weaver. Before he left to join the King's men, he sent me across the county for more wool. By the time I returned, all the men of the village had gone! A week I've been hiding out here.'

'But there's no point in staying. The longer you're here, the more chance there is of you being caught.'

'I can't leave,' Seth said quietly. 'My mother and little sister must be trapped in there with the others. Besides, now they've killed my friend Jethro . . .'

'So that was Jethro!' Ginger cried. 'I knew he didn't escape through the back window and skulk off to find food. He was really trying to rescue the others!'

'Of course he was, what are you babbling about?'

'When the war ends,' Ginger said, very seriously,

'you must write the full story of what happened here.'

'Me? Write?' Seth laughed. 'I've no letters, I can neither read nor write.'

'Then you'll have to learn, or tell it to somebody who can do it for you.'

'If I live long enough,' Seth said ruefully. 'As it is, I'll be lucky to get away with my life.'

'Oh, you *will* escape,' Ginger said firmly.

'You're an odd one and no mistake!' Seth grinned in spite of himself. 'How you can be certain of such things is beyond my understanding.'

'Take my word for it. But I've got to go now.'

'Not until I say!' Seth said, grabbing Ginger by the collar. 'I still have doubts about you.'

The shouting in the churchyard grew louder. The soldiers, who had piled up mounds of straw against the great wooden door and beneath all the church windows, had lit them with their torches. The flames hungrily lapped up the dry straw.

Seth was astonished. 'Surely they're not trying to smoke them out?'

'Worse than that,' Ginger said, grimly, as they watched soldiers pitching piles of burning straw in through the open windows.

Seth turned on Ginger. 'This is your doing. When you said they'd burn the people in the church, that was no prophesy but a spell you'd cast over the soldiers!'

Although he was frightened, Ginger couldn't help a brief smile. 'I'm not the son of a witch, or a wizard! I'm an ordinary boy like you, but I know they want to destroy the evidence of what they've done to Jethro.' Seth leapt towards the wall, but this time it was

Ginger's turn to hold him. 'Stay down! There's nothing you can do about it.'

'But my mother and little Ruth!'

'There's nothing you can do,' Ginger said earnestly, 'you'd be killed by the soldiers the moment you got over this wall. You must stay here. You're the only witness, the only person who knows the truth about what happened here tonight.'

Although Ginger knew Seth believed him, it was heartbreaking to see the agony of the poor boy's face as he was forced to watch.

The fire spread quickly through the church as it caught furniture, bedding and even clothes. They could hear horrifying screams coming from the people trapped inside as they fought, unsuccessfully, to quench it.

One soldier advanced towards his Colonel carrying the lifeless body of Jethro and, though the two boys could not hear what he said, the Colonel's response rang out clear enough: 'Pitch him in to fry with the rest!'

Ginger watched in horror as the soldier strode forward and heartlessly tossed Jethro's limp body through one of the windows into the growing inferno. He was not surprised to see tears streaking down Seth's grimy face.

He laid a hand on Seth's arm and said, 'Seth, when all this is over, remember what must be done.'

But writing an account was far from Seth's thoughts as he muttered through clenched teeth, 'I'll not forget what must be done to these fiends! Not 'til the day I die.'

'I have to go now,' Ginger said and quickly pressed the gold button, but to his amazement nothing happened and Seth had him by the wrist before he was able to try again.

'You'll stay and help me settle with them!'

'No, you don't understand, I can't!'

With a furious twist of his wrist Ginger loosened Seth's grip and backed away, just far enough to be able to give the button another long, hard push.

The sensation Ginger experienced was very peculiar. His body twitched and jerked, rather like trying to start a car with a flat battery and Ginger didn't know if he was going or staying.

Seth lunged forwards with his knife, but the wild punch Ginger swung happened to catch the boy on the wrist, knocking the weapon out of his grip. Before Seth could recover his balance, Ginger had picked up the knife, stuck it into his belt and given the gold button one last desperate press.

To his relief, Ginger at last felt himself going. But whereas before his departures had been swift, like being suddenly plunged into darkness, this time he felt himself being sucked slowly back towards his own time.

22

Double trouble

'I thought you were never coming back this time,' Clyde said.

'Me too,' Ginger said. 'The battery must be going.'

But Clyde wasn't listening. 'I've been freezing, hanging around here waiting.'

But Ginger couldn't stop shaking. 'I pressed and pressed the button, but nothing happened.' The journey back had been horrendous. Far from rushing through time, he'd crawled so slowly that several times Ginger was convinced that the battery had failed completely and he would never get back, abandoned in whatever century he happened to be passing through at the time. 'I really thought I was stuck.'

'What would I do then?' Clyde demanded angrily. 'Carry your sleeping body to your parents? "Oh, hello, Mrs Nutt. I've brought Ginger back. No, don't worry about him. I know he's in a coma right now, but he probably only has to live through a couple of centuries and he'll be as good as new when the battery gets invented!" I'd look a right idiot.'

'I'm sorry, Clyde, this isn't much fun for you. But this time I've brought you back a present. I met Seth, you remember, the boy who wrote the account of the siege that Lodge said was all wrong, but I know now for certain that he was telling the truth. Anyway, I've brought his hunting knife back with me.'

With a grand gesture, Ginger proudly pulled the knife from his belt, but Clyde collapsed in laughter. 'That's a perfectly ordinary sheath knife! You can buy one like that in any shop in the country.'

'It changed during the journey,' Ginger apologised.

'I'm getting sick of you and your journeys!' Clyde said, though Ginger noticed he still took the knife.

'Next time we'll find a safe place where we can't be found and go together.' Ginger could see that Clyde was far from happy. 'It'll be all right, honest. Look, if I can take your diagram and bring back a knife, then it'll be quite safe to take you too. Anything that's attached to me goes, like the kipper I hid in Janice's room.'

'Well, for a start, you can't tuck me in your belt and losing a kipper along the way wouldn't have mattered, but you're not accidentally dropping me off somewhere between here and 1644, thanks all the same!' Clyde said firmly. 'Besides, aren't you forgetting something? Nobody can go nowhere until you get a new battery for that thing.'

'True,' Ginger agreed. 'But I think we've got some in the shop. Come on, it's getting cold hanging round here.'

'Tell me about it!' Clyde grumbled, as they wandered off back to Ginger's.

But, when they got back, there was no time to look for a battery.

Mum met them at the door looking very upset. 'Where've you two been?'

'Only down to the churchyard. Why, Mum, what's the matter?'

'It's Gran. She's wandered off again.'

Twice they'd had to rescue her from a supermarket. The manager wasn't very pleased the second time because she'd filled four shopping trolleys to overflowing with groceries, which had to be laboriously returned to the shelves. Also, when the manager wouldn't let her out without paying, she'd burst a family-sized selection pack of crisps over his head.

Once the police picked her up. She had no money with her and was only dressed in her nightdress and slippers, but she'd somehow managed to stop a car, convince the driver it was an emergency and he'd driven her to the City Infirmary fifteen miles away!

'We'll help, won't we, Clyde?'

Clyde nodded.

'Dad's coming too while Janice looks after the shop.'

'Trust her to get the easy job.'

'Ginger! This is no time for bickering. We've got to find Gran as soon as possible. It's getting colder every minute and she's only wearing that thin red dress.'

Dad came out to join them. 'Oh, good, you're back.'

'Yes, I'd have been back quicker only my battery's run down,' Ginger said, giving Clyde, who burst out laughing, a firm nudge in the ribs.

'What on earth are you on about?' Dad demanded.

'Nothing, Dad.'

'Right, now there's four of us, it'll be quicker if we split up and take different streets. Your mum and me will do both ends of the main road, Clyde you go round by Khartoum Street down as far as the canal . . .'

'Oh,' Mum gasped. 'I hope she hasn't gone wandering along the towpath in the dark.'

'It's just a precaution,' Dad said, trying to calm her. 'Ginger, you go up the roads around Battlefield Terrace as far as the park.'

'Okay, but what it we don't find her?'

Mum was close to tears. 'Don't say that, Ginger.'

Dad slipped an arm round Mum's shoulder. 'He only meant, what do we do next? Once you've searched all round your area come back here in half an hour and we'll decide. She can't have got far on her bad feet.'

As he worked his way up Battlefield Terrace, Ginger looked in all the gardens, but there was no sign of Gran.

Ginger searched the roads round about, still no luck. None of the few people he met on the way had noticed an old lady in a red dress.

By the time he reached the park, Ginger had almost given up hope. Then a brilliant idea struck him. Although there wasn't much power left in the watch, surely it would be safe to go back half an hour? Then he might be able to see where Gran went and either stop her, or persuade her to come back. Anyway, it wouldn't matter if he got stuck half an hour back, he'd still be able to return to the shop and fit a new battery.

Not wanting anyone to find him collapsed on the pavement, Ginger went into the bus shelter and sat on the bench while he adjusted the figures and pressed the gold button.

Because of the weak battery and the short time he had to travel, Ginger felt little more than a shudder.

The kind Gran often referred to as somebody having walked over her grave.

But Ginger was rather shocked when he tried to get up. His legs were either missing, or invisible. But, having hauled himself up by clutching the walls of the bus shelter, Ginger discovered he could still move, hovering a few metres above the ground, and by flapping his arms he could propel himself forwards, like a bird flying, or perhaps more like a fish swimming through air.

'Dratted battery!' he said. 'But there's nothing I can do about it now and I'll only be here for a few minutes while I look for Gran.'

He was almost back at the shop and there'd still been no sign of Gran. But then, as he turned into Adventure Street, the side door opened and out she popped.

Without thinking, Ginger called out, 'Hi, Gran, where are you off to?'

Gran turned and looked at the top half of her grandson's body, without legs, floating above the pavement, but this rather strange sight didn't seem to bother her in the least. Probably because Gran's mind was always performing this kind of mental gymnastics! 'I've often said, lad, most of the time you're only half there!'

Ginger grinned. 'It's a bit cold out here for you, Gran, without a coat. Let's get back inside where it's warm.'

'Oh, no,' Gran said, very firmly. 'I can't do that. I have to go and feed the ducks in the park.'

'The ducks are asleep, Gran. Besides, you haven't

brought any bread.'

Gran got close to him and whispered, 'That's only an excuse. Really, I'm going to meet Ronald. But it's a secret, they don't want me to see any more of him, so you mustn't let on to anyone.'

'Well, if you must go,' Ginger said, happy that now he knew where she was, he would be able to bring her back before she came to any harm. 'You'd better put my anorak around your shoulders to keep out the cold.'

Because Gran so readily accepted the idea of him swimming along in thin air beside her, he quite forgot about his missing legs. But as they made their way back up Battlefield Terrace and reached The King's Head, a drunk swayed out and came face to face with Ginger, or half of him.

'I swear, I'll never have another drink as long as I live!' the man said.

'A good thing too!' Gran said and she stomped off leaving the man, sitting with his feet in the gutter. 'No good ever came from drinking alcohol,' Gran added. 'I persuaded Ronald to join the Band of Hope and now he never touches anything stronger than lemonade.'

'Are you sure Ronald will be waiting for you, Gran? It's quite late.'

'He'll be there, never you fear!' Gran said, but when they reached the duck pond, as they walked round the edge, they could see in the moonlight, all the benches were empty.

Gran sighed and looked very upset. 'He promised he'd meet me!'

'Never mind, Gran,' Ginger said gently. 'It's very

late, perhaps we ought to go home?'

But Gran, far from listening, was ringing her handkerchief in her hands. 'Pearls, you mark my words.'

'Who's Pearl?' Ginger asked.

But instead of replying, Gran just kept muttering, 'Pearls!' over and over again, and tears began to run down her cheeks.

Realising there was nothing he could do, but that he ought to get her back home out of the cold, he decided he'd better nip, or float, round to the bus shelter and try and get back into his whole body. 'You stay here, Gran, I'll be back in a minute.'

But when Ginger reached the bus shelter and pressed the button, after the briefest of tremors, Ginger found he was looking at himself. There were now two of him. Or to be more exact, one and a half! What was worse, as he glanced at his watch, the figures faded to nothing as the battery power completely fizzled out.

'Now what do I do? I ought to get back to Gran in case she wanders off.'

He had hardly said it before the legs seemed to respond. His legs got up and carried his sleeping upper half towards the park!

'Hang on a minute! Wait for me!' Ginger shouted, swimming furiously so as not to lose track of himself.

23

Beside himself

Only Ginger worried about how, or if, he'd ever be able to get back together with himself. Gran accepted the arrival in the park of one and a half Gingers, as the most normal thing in the world.

She only glanced at his closed eyes and said, 'Sometimes, our Ginger, you're a dozy devil!'

But for both of them, it was important to get home to the shop quickly, without meeting anyone along the way, if possible.

'Gran,' he said gently, 'I think we ought to go home now. The others will be worried.'

'Mum will,' Gran agreed, though Ginger wasn't certain whether she meant her mother, or his.

Everything went quite well until they were at the bottom of Battlefield Terrace when a woman with two small children came out of their gate and began walking up towards them.

'Oh, no!' Ginger gasped. 'They mustn't see me like this!'

But he flapped his arms so hard trying to dodge into one of the gardens and hide behind the hedge, that instead of moving sideways, he suddenly floated upwards and hovered at first floor level.

'Wicked!' said Ginger. 'They'll never see me in the dark up here.'

But at that moment a light came on in the bedroom alongside him and Ginger was so well lit, he might have been a star trapeze act, caught in a spotlight, high above a circus.

The little boy with his mother called out from beneath Ginger, 'Is it a bird? Is it a plane? No, it's Superman! Look, Mum, up there!'

But luckily for Ginger the boy's mother was in too much hurry. She jerked the lad's hand so hard he almost tripped, saying irritably, 'Don't talk so daft and keep up, we're late enough as it is!'

They'd hardly turned the corner when a sudden scream pierced the night. Ginger swung round to find Debbie Catling, from his class, staring at him from the brilliantly lit bedroom. She'd come upstairs to change and was half undressed.

'You disgusting beast!' she screamed and ran from the room, shouting, 'Dad! There's a Peeping Tom outside my bedroom window.'

To escape, Ginger flapped his arms so violently that he had to catch hold of the Catlings' television aerial to avoid floating away into the night sky. Then he hid, squatting down on the roof ridge behind the chimney stack.

Below him a door opened and Ginger heard a man's voice saying, 'There's nobody out here.'

'But I saw him!' Debbie protested. 'I could have sworn it was that horrible Ginger Nutt from the paper shop. He was right outside my window.'

'How could he be?' Mr Catling demanded. 'He'd

need a ladder for that and there isn't one out here!'

'But he saw me with almost nothing on!' Debbie wailed.

'Aye, well, I've told you before,' Mr Catling said unkindly, 'the things you wear, don't cover much up, even when you're fully dressed. Now clear off, you and your imagination, you've made me miss the pools coupon check!'

When all was quiet, Ginger tried to get down off the roof, only to discover it wasn't as easy as getting up.

Whichever way he flapped his arms, he either went higher, or almost fell off the roof. Eventually he found the best method was to haul himself, hand over hand down the drainpipe. Part way down, he lost his grip and plummeted towards the ground. Instinctively, as he fell, Ginger spread his arms and to his astonishment he was no longer falling, but soaring like an eagle.

'This is great!' Ginger laughed.

With a little practice, he discovered that by tilting his balance to either side, he could steer quite well.

'I could get to like this! But I suppose I'd better catch up with Gran before I lose her again.'

Getting up speed, Ginger performed a neat slalom in and out of the lampposts as he flew after Gran and his other self, who had walked on without him. A group of lads coming in the opposite direction, forced Ginger to lead them through some back alleys taking them past Mr Cumpsty's dimly lit shop.

Gran headed straight to the door.

'No, Gran,' Ginger said, catching her by the arm. 'We can't go in there.'

Gran looked quite angry. 'You said we were going

home, Ronald. Why do you keep changing your mind?'

'But this isn't your home.'

Gran drew herself up. 'Not my home? I've lived here all my life, Ronald, as well you know!'

Ginger wasn't sure how to get out of this situation. Much as he would have enjoyed going into the shop and scaring the living daylights out of the old skinflint, he knew Mr Cumpsty would certainly tell the whole town.

'Look, Gran, Mum will be worried.'

'I know,' Gran agreed, 'she thinks I've only been out to feed the ducks. She doesn't know I went to meet you, Ronald.'

Ginger crossed his fingers and hoped if he played along that might do the trick. 'So, now we've met,' he said, ignoring the flicker of confusion which passed across the old lady's face, 'why don't we go for a little walk?'

Gran looked back uncertainly towards the shop door. 'I'm not sure. I ought to go in.' She looked more closely at Ginger. 'Are you really Ronald? You only look a bit like him, but Ronald had more about him than you somehow.'

So did Ginger, once, Ginger thought to himself. 'We'll only be gone a minute. Nobody need ever know.'

To his enormous relief, Gran gave in, followed him down the road and they soon rounded the corner into Adventure Street.

Ginger hadn't yet worked out how he was going to get his hands on a new battery, not while the gimlet-eyed Janice was minding the shop, but he let Gran in through the side door. 'You pop inside, I won't be a minute.'

He held his breath, expecting her to refuse, but instead she smiled. 'I'd better cut your sandwiches for work,' she said.

'That's right, but don't cut too many,' he added, glancing at his missing half, 'I'm not sure I've got anywhere to put them!'

Hardly had he closed the door than he heard voices and footsteps coming towards him. It was Mum and Dad returning with Clyde. Ginger grabbed the arm of his other self and shoved so hard that it fell behind the low wall which surrounded next door's front yard. Then he positioned himself behind the wall so that nobody would notice the rather crucial absence of his legs!

'Where've you been, Ginger?' Dad asked. 'We arranged to meet here half an hour ago. It's worrying enough we have to go out looking for Gran, without having to search for you too!'

'I found Gran,' Ginger cut in, 'and brought her back, but she couldn't walk very fast. She's in the house.'

'Oh, thanks, Ginger!' Mum said and she rushed inside to find her mother.

Dad was about to follow, but on the top step he turned back towards Ginger. 'What are you doing in Mrs Khan's yard?'

'Just doing a bit of tidying up for her,' Ginger lied.

'Aye, you're not such a bad lad. But don't wander off, it's nearly tea-time.'

'I might have to pop up to the bus shelter.'

'What on earth for?' Dad asked.

'Oh, nothing,' Ginger said innocently, 'I just left something behind.'

'Well, don't be long, son, and thanks for your help, Clyde.'

'You're welcome, Mr Nutt,' Clyde said.

The moment Ginger's father had closed the door he asked Ginger, 'What *are* you doing behind that wall?'

'I've got a bit of a problem,' Ginger admitted and did a press push-up on the wall, revealing the absence of his legs.

The smile vanished from Clyde's face and he looked as he was about to throw up. Finally he stammered, 'How did you get chopped in half?'

'It's the battery in my watch,' Ginger explained. 'I went back in time to look for Gran but only just made it and I could only get halfway back before the power ran out.'

Ginger looked so sorry for himself that Clyde couldn't help laughing. 'You're only half the man you used to be!'

'Very funny!' Ginger said bitterly. 'But as a matter of fact, you're wrong.' Heaving his other self up beside him, he added, triumphantly, 'I'm nearly twice the man you are!'

Clyde fell about. 'Oh, pull yourself together!'

24

Gran's Great Sorrow

'Mum, who was Pearl?' Ginger asked. It was long after tea. The new battery had been put in the watch and he was none the worse for his temporary split personality. Gran had gone to bed early, to rest after her expedition.

'Pearl?' Mum, whose hands were deep in the soapy washing-up water, looked mystified. 'I don't know anybody called Pearl. Don't just stand there, wipe some of these dishes.'

Ginger picked up a tea towel and slowly wiped a plate. 'When I was in the park with Gran, she said she was expecting to meet Ronald there and when he didn't turn up she got very upset and went on about Pearl's something or other.'

Light dawned on Mum's face. 'Oh, the pearls! It isn't somebody's name – it was a string of pearls!' Mum sighed. 'They were the cause of Gran's Sorrow.'

'How do you mean?'

'If you keep rubbing that plate you'll have the pattern off,' she rebuked.

Ginger grabbed another plate, anxious not to let Mum off the hook. 'But what *is* her Sorrow?'

'I don't even know if it's true. She never talked about it when I was a girl. It's only come up these last few years, since her mind's got confused and it's so scrambled up I never know what to believe.'

'Ronald's part of it though, isn't he?'

'Yes, he was an old flame of your gran's. It was all a long time ago, during the First World War.'

'Go on,' Ginger urged.

'Your great-grandfather was quite well off. They had a grocer's shop. It was where Mr Cumpsty's shop is now.'

Ginger instantly stopped wiping, a creepy tingle running down the back of his neck. 'That was their shop?'

'Yes. Of course, it was a lot smarter then than it is now.'

So the man who'd chased after him for stealing biscuits must have been his own great-grandfather! No wonder Gran had wanted to go into Mr Cumpsty's on their way back from the park.

'But he wasn't rich when he married your great-grandmother. He couldn't even afford an engagement ring, but he promised as soon as he could afford it, he'd buy her a double row of pearls to make up for it. Which he did. Ginger, you've stopped drying again!'

'Sorry, go on.'

'By all accounts they were very expensive and really beautiful.'

'But what's all this to do with Ronald?'

'I'm coming to that. Gran and Ronald were childhood sweethearts. Ronald lived next door and he grew up with Gran. Even when they were little, they always said they were going to get married and when they got older they began courting.'

'Courting?'

'Going out together,' Mum explained. 'That's what they called it in those days. Your great-grandfather wasn't very pleased. He didn't think Ronald was good enough for the daughter of a man who'd made his way in the world. He'd decided Gran should marry Harold. Harold, according to Gran, was a smarmy, eldest son of the local fishmonger. Gran says he was a great deal older than her, smelled of haddock and she'd have nothing to do with him. So it was stalemate. Gran didn't want Harold and your great-grandfather wouldn't give permission for her to get engaged to Ronald, let alone marry him. So they made up their minds to wait until they were both twenty-one and wouldn't need anybody's permission.'

Ginger found it very hard to think of the confused, old lady, his grandmother, being part of some great love story.

'But they never got the chance. The First World War was on, Ronald got called up into the army. Your great-grandfather hoped things would fizzle out between them while they were apart. They didn't though. While Ronald was doing his training, they wrote to each other almost every day and just before he set off for France with his regiment, Ronald came home on what they called embarkation leave. Her father forbade them to meet, but they did. She used to sneak out of the house and they'd meet in the park.'

'By the duck pond, Gran told me tonight, but where do the pearls come in?'

'After Ronald left they discovered the lovely string of pearls, your great-grandmother's pride and joy, was missing. They turned over the whole house, couldn't find them anywhere and her father swore Ronald had stolen them.' Mum pulled the plug out of the sink and watched the soapy water run away.

'But how could he if he wasn't allowed in the house?'

'He was once. The night before Ronald set off, Great-grandfather relented. They knew what a dreadful war it was and these young lads were going out to fight for king and country. So Ronald and some of the other lads from round about, who'd all joined up at the same time, were invited for a bit of a party. During the party Ronald had disappeared and Great-grandfather thought that was when he had stolen the necklace.'

'But when the war was over,' Ginger said, 'they could find out what really happened.'

Mum shook her head. 'None of them came back. Not one. It was said that they never fired a shot. They were all killed by the heavy German shelling soon after they arrived in the trenches a week before the Battle of Passchendaele. So, Gran not only lost the great love of her life, but her father would never again allow his name to be mentioned.'

'Poor Gran.'

Mum said, drying her hands, 'Now you know as much as I've been able to piece together about her Great Sorrow.'

'Was the pearl necklace never found?'

'Never. It was always a complete mystery, but your great-grandfather, my grandfather, swore until the day he died that Ronald was responsible.'

That night Ginger was woken by loud noises coming from downstairs. He tracked them down to the kitchen and when he threw open the door, there was Gran surrounded by a pile of baking tins which had fallen out of the cupboard.

'I'm baking a cake,' she announced proudly.

'But it's three o'clock on Sunday morning, Gran.'

'The better the day, the better the deed,' she said, breaking every available egg into a basin. 'It's Ronald's birthday tomorrow.'

'How old's Ronald going to be?'

'Seventeen.'

'What's he like?'

'You've seen him often enough,' she said. She was trying to tip flour into the weighing pan of the scales, but her hands trembled so much under the weight of the bag that most of it spread over the kitchen unit in a cloud.

'I bet you've got a photo of him.'

Gran looked sharply at Ginger. 'You mustn't tell!'

'No, I promise.'

Gran wiped her floury hands on her apron as she went over to the kitchen table where she'd left her precious photograph album. It was bound in dark, tooled, heavily padded leather and when it was open it gave off a musty smell. The pages were quite thick and decorated with intricate floral patterns in faded red, yellow and green. The edges of the pages and the surrounds to each of the sepia-coloured prints they held, were slightly bevelled and shiny with gilt.

'Who wrote all this?' Ginger asked, pointing at the

names, and sometimes dates, written beneath the pictures in jet-black, spidery copperplate.

'I don't remember, dear.'

She turned several pages until Ginger stopped her at a familiar face, bristling with side-whiskers. 'Who's that?'

'My father,' she said, automatically slipping into her habit of referring to everyone as if they were still living. 'He doesn't approve of Ronald. This one's my mother.'

Ginger noticed that the grim-looking woman was proudly wearing the double row of pearls for her photograph.

Then Gran turned the page to reveal another familiar face and without thinking he cried out, 'Alice!'

Gran turned to him and said, 'Yes, dear?'

For the first time it dawned on Ginger that Alice, the pretty girl with the bright blue eyes and red hair who'd served them in the shop, was Gran when young.

'Where's Ronald then?' he asked quickly.

Gran gave him a mischievous smile, glanced round to confirm they were alone, and carefully slid down her own photograph within the cardboard frame to reveal another hidden behind it, of a young man. 'That's him,' she said lovingly. 'That's my Ronald.'

Ginger couldn't see what all the fuss was about. Apart from having rather intense, dark eyes, there was nothing particularly special about the slim young man, with greased-down hair, who gazed out shyly from the photograph. But Ginger didn't think he'd ever understand what girls saw in most men. Look at the boys Janice drooled over! It would have been different if they'd been Arnold Schwarzenegger!

Gran was gazing so adoringly at the photograph that Ginger, to avoid her bursting into more tears, whispered, 'I think someone's coming, better hide it.'

Gran tucked the photograph away in its secret hiding place and turned the page. The next photograph was more in Ginger's line! Unlike the others he'd seen, all stiff, formal studio portraits, complete with aspidistra, this was a slightly fuzzy snapshot of a group of young boys desperately trying to look casual, yet obviously proud as punch of their new uniforms.

'That was taken while they were all on leave,' Gran said.

Ginger hastily memorised the date under the picture, 20 June 1917. 'Was that the day they went back?' he asked casually.

'Oh, no. This was taken soon after they arrived, they didn't leave until the following Monday.'

Which meant, Ginger did some quick calculations, if what Mum said was true, the farewell party was held on the evening of Saturday the twenty-sixth. Then he leant forward and peered more closely at the picture. 'Ronald isn't in this, is he?'

Gran shook her head and pointed at the others one by one, naming them as she went: 'That's Sam and George. Reggie from round the corner and that horrible Alfred out of Mafeking Street. And look at this one!' she said with a laugh.

Ginger looked at the face Gran was pointing at. He might have been looking into a tiny mirror. 'Who's that?'

'Cousin Jack. He was a proper card was Jack. I often

25

Swine before pearls?

'All we have to do is tie this rope round our ankles. The way we did for the three-legged race. It's perfectly safe,' Ginger explained to Clyde, for the third time. 'Nothing can go wrong.'

Although Clyde was desperate to travel with Ginger on his next expedition, he would have liked a simpler, shorter journey than the one Ginger had planned, which was to go back to 1917 and get involved in a dodgy-sounding scheme for solving Gran's Great Sorrow.

'I don't want to end up with no legs, like you did!' Clyde said.

'We've been through all that,' Ginger said. 'Probably an old battery that had been in for years. That can't happen now we've replaced it. Look, all I want you to do is hide outside the house with me, wait for Jack and then follow Ronald if he leaves the house. I'm the one doing the difficult part, I've got to go inside.'

'It's separating while we're there that bothers me most,' Clyde admitted. 'I think that's dead risky.'

'Not if we arrange a time and place to meet up and travel back together.'

'I'm hardly likely to leave without you, am I? Okay,

think you're the image of him.'

'Aren't I just,' Ginger agreed, as an idea began to form of a way of sorting out Gran's Great Sorrow.

I suppose I'm ready,' Clyde agreed reluctantly. 'But I still wish we didn't have to go from here.'

They were squatting in the dark amongst a clump of Christmas trees in the corner of the churchyard. 'This is the only place I could think of where nobody's likely to find us once we've passed out. Come on, we've wasted enough time, let's get on with it. Have you brought the bag?'

Clyde pulled part of a nylon mesh shopping bag out of his pocket. He wasn't looking forward to that part of Ginger's plan either!

'Right, I'll tie this piece of rope round our ankles.'

'*I'll* do that!' Clyde said, snatching the rope from Ginger. 'I don't want to get dropped off in the middle of World War Two because one of your granny knots slips undone.'

Clyde tied the rope tight enough to cut off all flow of blood to their feet and Ginger adjusted his watch, ready to take them back to the evening of the soldiers' farewell party, 26 June 1917.

As Clyde finished the knot he couldn't help laughing at Ginger. 'You look a right lemon in that uniform!'

Ginger had borrowed Mugsy Tanner's army cadet uniform, in the hope that when they arrived in 1917 it would have been transformed into something like a proper First World War army outfit, or close enough for him not to stand out in the crowd.

The problem was that Mugsy was taller and a good deal fatter than Ginger. The cuffs dangled over Ginger's wrists, there was a pleat of material gathered under his belt and he kept tripping over the trousers, even though he'd turned them up using a stapler!

'It's the best I could do,' Ginger said. 'Are you ready?'

'As ready as I'll ever be.' Clyde shut his eyes and braced himself.

'Right, here goes!'

When Ginger pressed the button, instead of instantly charging off through time, he first felt himself being jerked forwards and then tugged back again. Probably because of Clyde's extra weight, it was more like a railway engine attempting to move a line of heavy trucks.

And even when they had got started, far from hurtling forwards, feet first, because they were joined at the ankle, they rolled over and over each other, like a crazy bobsleigh team charging down the Cresta Run.

'Are you all right?' Ginger shouted above the roar of rushing wind.

'Awesome!' Clyde grinned from above him. 'I never expected it to be this good. Wheee!' he shouted and rolled over, weightlessly like a free-fall parachutist, twisting Ginger over with him.

Moments later they collided with the usual invisible time wall and found themselves lying beside a tombstone outside the darkened church. Having untied the rope, which Ginger carefully coiled and kept for later use, they hared off towards the town as fast as Ginger's trouser legs would allow.

'Isn't it weird,' Clyde said, jogging alongside Ginger, 'when you sort of know everywhere and yet it's all different?'

They stopped in a doorway opposite the grocer's shop. The shop itself was closed and in darkness, but chinks of light escaped through cracks in the curtained bedroom windows above.

'Later on, this would be a good spot to watch for Ronald coming out of the house,' Ginger suggested. 'But first, if my plan's going to work, we must stop Jack going to the party.'

They crept down the entry which ran alongside the shop. As they reached a brilliantly lit, uncurtained window, Ginger cautiously peered over the sill.

'This must be the sitting room,' Ginger whispered.

'Anybody in there?'

'A few people.'

'What about Jack?'

'I can't see him.'

The entry turned a right angle, to run along the back of the terrace of shops, and on the corner Ginger and Clyde found a small, unlocked outbuilding.

'If we hide in here we'll be able to see everybody as they arrive,' Ginger said, leaving the door open a crack.

The building was almost filled by a mound of dusty shopfittings and a delivery bike with a huge wicker basket on the front. The boys were hardly inside before they heard echoing footsteps coming along the entry towards them.

'Is it Jack?' Clyde asked, trying to peer over Ginger's shoulder and out through the crack in the door.

Ginger waited until the people walked through the light spilling out from the sitting-room window. 'No, I think they're Sam and George,' he whispered uncertainly, forced to rely on his memory of the photograph in Gran's album.

Next to arrive were Ronald, Reggie and 'horrible Alfred out of Mafeking Street'. There was no mistaking Alfred with his greasy, black hair and moth-eaten moustache.

'Suppose Jack doesn't come on his own!' Clyde murmured.

'Never mind that,' Ginger hissed back, 'haven't you noticed? I thought they'd all be in uniform, but they're wearing suits. I'll stick out like a cat in a bird cage!'

'Why don't you go back home and change?' Clyde asked with a laugh, but his expression changed to horror as Ginger pulled up his oversized cuff to get at his watch. 'Hey, Ginger, that was supposed to be a joke! Don't leave me here!'

'I'm not going to, don't get your knickers in a twist!' Ginger said. 'I was only checking the time.'

'Ssh! I can hear somebody else coming. Is this one Jack?'

Ginger peered out through the doorway. 'I'm not sure.'

'Does he look like you?'

Ginger waited until the young man walked through the pool of light. 'Yes, it's him! Let's do it!'

The minute Jack passed the outbuilding, Clyde and Ginger sneaked out behind him. As Jack opened the back gate, Clyde whipped out the bag he'd brought, which had turned into a straw shopping bag and whipped it over his head.

'Hey up! What's this then – Blind Man's Buff?' Jack's muffled voice asked. 'Is that you, Sam? No, I bet it's Reggie!'

'No, but we're not going to hurt you,' Ginger said,

tying some of the rope around Jack's arms and tugging what was left like a dog's lead. 'Follow me.'

'Where are you taking me?' Jack asked.

'You'll be perfectly safe,' Clyde said as they went back into the outbuilding.

'We want you to stay here for a while and keep quiet. It's just a little joke we're playing on the others,' Ginger said. 'Alice always says you like jokes.'

'Oh, I do,' Jack said nervously.

'Good, then sit down on the floor.'

Jack did as he was told and Ginger tied his ankles together. 'We'll come back and let you out, don't worry,' Ginger said and they went back out into the entry and shut the door. 'Right, go, Clyde!'

'But when do we meet up again?' Clyde asked anxiously.

Ginger checked his watch. 'It's half-past eight now. Let's say, back here at ten o'clock. That should give us plenty of time and remember, once Ronald's out of the house, you stick with him and if he tries to come back any earlier, you'll have to find a way to stop him.'

'Okay, I'll do my best. See you!'

As Clyde walked back up the entry to take up his position, Ginger nervously ran a hand through his hair, entered the yard and walked up to the back door to join the party.

'Here I go!'

26

Hitting the right note

'Hello, Jack,' a voice boomed out the moment Ginger stepped through the door into the back kitchen. This was Sam. 'Hey,' he said, 'it's not a fancy-dress party!'

'My suit's at the cleaners,' Ginger apologised.

'And you've had your hair cut,' Sam said. 'Makes you look even younger. Get yourself a glass of beer and go through, the others are all in the sitting room.'

Ginger ignored the beer and walked through. This was the moment he'd privately been dreading. He was very scared at the prospect of seeing his relatives.

When he'd first met his great-grandfather and his grandmother, they'd simply been people running a grocer's shop. Now he knew who they really were it seemed quite different, especially as he was about to deliberately try and fool them into thinking he was somebody he wasn't! Perhaps it was safer to concentrate on being Jack and keep thinking of them as the grocer and his assistant, because if they weren't fooled, as Sam had been, then his plan could never work.

But he needn't have worried. The moment he entered the room, everyone greeted him as Jack and made fun of his ill-fitting uniform, or his haircut, just as Sam had. After that the party went quite well and

Ginger didn't have much difficulty passing himself off as Jack because whatever he said, even if he made mistakes, they just accepted that as being 'typical Jack, playing the fool as usual!'

But Ginger knew he had to keep alert until he'd found out who the thief was. At nine o'clock he was the only person in the room who noticed Ronald, who'd been keeping well away from Alice, slip out of the house. Five minutes later, Alice followed.

Now, this is when the fun really starts, Ginger thought, positioning himself near the door, so that anybody leaving the room had to pass him. But though many people passed him, most only went to the kitchen and came back with more beer.

'How are you keeping then, young Jack?' Alice's father asked. 'Ready to do your bit in France?'

'I reckon,' Ginger replied and then whispered in the man's ear, 'I don't know if I should say, but have you noticed, Ronald's disappeared.'

The old man's face clouded over. 'Disappeared?'

'Yes,' Ginger said, 'I don't know why, but I think he went upstairs.'

'Upstairs?' The man stormed out and Ginger congratulated himself on establishing Ronald's alibi, especially when the grocer returning saying, 'There's nobody up there, Jack.'

'I know,' Ginger said with a grin. 'Caught you there, didn't I?'

For a moment Ginger thought the man might explode, until he burst out laughing. 'You and your jokes, Jack!'

'Jack!' Reggie called out across the room. 'Come

over here, lad, we're going to have a sing-song.'

Ginger happily walked over to the piano with the others, ready to join in as best he could, but his happiness died abruptly when Reggie gave him a shove and said, 'Well, come on, sit down and play!'

'Who me?' Ginger gulped. If he touched the keys he was bound to be found out. He'd only had lessons for six months before his piano teacher begged Mum not to send Ginger any more! The way Ginger played, proved beyond any doubt he had no sense of rhythm and was almost certainly tone-deaf!

George laughed. 'You're the only one that knows the latest tunes.'

Latest tunes? Ginger hadn't the least idea what was topping the charts in 1917!

'Hurry up!' Sam boomed, pushing Ginger on to the piano stool.

Amid much laughter, Ginger made a great show of pulling back his cuffs and cracking his fingers, the way he'd seen a mad pianist do it in a Bugs Bunny Cartoon, while desperately trying to remember any tune he'd ever learned.

Eventually, to more laughter, he launched into a clumsy version of chopsticks, but they wouldn't let him off. 'Play something proper we can all sing.'

'Well, you've asked for it!' he said and fell into a diabolical rendering of a classical piece he'd been forced to learn, 'Für Elise,' the only other music he could remember.

Unfortunately this was the very last piece he had learned. But as the wrong notes clanged out, in amongst enough of the right ones for them to be able to recognise the tune, everybody took it as just another of Jack's great jokes and roared with laughter.

'Play "It's a long way to Tipperary",' Sam boomed.

'All right, you start,' Ginger said quickly.

Sam obliged with a chorus. By the second line, everyone had joined in without waiting for the piano and Ginger got up and pretended to conduct. It was as they were going through it for the second time, that Ginger noticed Alfred hovering self-consciously by the door, playing with his weedy moustache. Next time Ginger looked he'd gone.

'I need another drink,' Ginger excused himself to George, and left them singing, while he went in search of Alfred.

The kitchen was deserted and although Ginger popped out into the back yard, Alfred wasn't there either.

As Ginger stealthily made his way upstairs, the singers moved on to 'Pack up your troubles in your old kit bag'. He'd reached the landing when the singing suddenly grew louder as someone below opened the door.

Ginger pressed himself flat against the wall, but nobody came, the sitting-room door closed again and Ginger continued his search.

Having tried all the other rooms, he found Alfred, rather as he'd expected, bending over a dressing table and at the very moment Ginger peeped through the crack by the hinges, Alfred was in the act of slipping the string of pearls into his pocket.

Right, thought Ginger, now we know!

Ginger crept downstairs and hid in the kitchen,

expecting Alfred to rejoin the others, but instead he went down the corridor towards the darkened shop. Cautiously Ginger followed him on tiptoe and crouched behind the huge counter amongst the piles of red and blue paper bags.

With no light it was very difficult to see what Alfred was up to, apart from the fact he was fiddling about with some packets on one of the shelves. Then by the dim headlights of a car which roared by outside, Ginger plainly saw the silhouette of Alfred, slipping the pearls into the packet he'd opened and replacing it on the shelf.

'The crafty devil!' Ginger muttered after Alfred had gone. 'He doesn't want to have the pearls on him in case anybody realises they've been stolen. So he hides them in here and he can come back and collect them tomorrow when the shop's open!'

Ginger nipped round the counter, found the packet at the back of a line of identical packets of suet and drew out the string of pearls Alfred had stuffed inside.

'Now to set Gran's mind at rest!' he said. Pocketing the pearls and unbolting the shop door, Ginger let himself out into the deserted street. This was the part of the plan he'd never mentioned to Clyde and he'd always kept his fingers crossed behind his back, when promising Clyde he wouldn't go back without him!

It was ten to ten, Clyde was due back any minute. Ginger pressed the button and found himself outside Mr Cumpsty's. He ran full tilt back home and then crept upstairs to knock on Gran's door. She was sitting in an armchair at the foot of the bed, knitting a sock in khaki wool. When Ginger went in, she looked up and smiled. 'Hello, Jack, how smart you look in your uniform.'

'Thanks, Alice,' Ginger said, thinking it was best to keep up the pretence.

'You'll all be off tomorrow and I haven't finished these socks for Ronald.'

'Alice, I just wanted you to know, the pearls are safe.' He pulled them out of his pocket and held them out for her to see.

She dropped the knitting on her lap and took the pearls in her hands. It was as if years of worry dropped from her shoulders and the worry lines seemed to fade from her face. 'Oh, I'm so pleased!' she said. 'Father was certain they'd never be seen again and Mother was so fond of them!'

'It was Alfred who took them, not Ronald at I saw him do it.'

'I knew it wasn't Ronald! That wicked Alfred! Fancy letting Ronald take the blame – I always knew Alfred was up to no good.'

Ginger reached out to take back the pearls, but Gran wouldn't release them. 'No,' she said firmly, 'I'm not letting them out of my sight again.'

'But you must!' Ginger began to panic, if he couldn't take the pearls back to 1917 with him, then they'd still appear to be stolen. 'I've got to give them back to your father.'

'I'll do that,' she said, holding them behind her.

'No, you mustn't. Otherwise they might think you have been given them by Ronald and he really had stolen them!'

Gran considered this for a moment before reluctantly

handing them back to Ginger. 'Yes, you're probably right, besides I'd only lose them. I seem to keep forgetting where I put things. Where's my knitting?'

Without thinking, he said, 'On the chair, Gran.'

She gave him an odd look, but Ginger had gone before she could say anything.

Moments later, he was back outside Mr Cumpsty's. He pressed the button and swiftly slipped into the grocer's shop. He rebolted the door, replaced the pearls in the suet packet, crept out through the house and into the back yard and ran round to the front of the shop. It was five to ten, time was getting very short. He pressed the button again to return to his own time and, his fingers trembling, reset the watch for the morning of Monday 28 June 1917.

Still blinking in the sudden burst of daylight, Ginger practically landed on top of another man, also in army uniform, whom he knocked flat.

'Where did you spring from?' the man demanded, angrily picking himself up.

It was in the moment it took for the man to dust himself down, that Ginger realised, first of all, that he was a grown-up version of Will, whom he'd last met dressed in rags when they bought the biscuits, and secondly, whereas Ginger was wearing a private's uniform, those stripes on Will's arm showed he was a sergeant!

'Sorry,' Ginger said.

'Never mind sorry, soldier, what about a salute?' Will began and then his tone changed to recognition. 'Jack! It's a good job it's you, otherwise I'd have you up on a charge for attacking a non-commissioned officer! Not to mention being improperly dressed. Where's your cap?'

'I didn't think I'd need it,' Ginger said in total honesty. 'I've only popped round to the shop before I set off for the station.'

Will's expression changed to one of sympathy. 'Off to the Front, aren't you?' Ginger nodded. 'Well, good luck, Jack, you'll certainly need it where you're going!'

With that, Will shook his hand and left.

Seconds later, Alfred came round the corner, heading for the shop and Ginger crossed the road to meet him. 'Hello, Alfred.'

Alfred looked slightly startled and a little guilty, but he managed to smile. 'Hello, Jack. I see you're ready for the off. Mum asked me to pop in for a couple of things before I go to the station.'

'Me too,' Ginger said, following Alfred into the shop.

But he began to wonder if Alfred had changed his mind, when he asked the grocer to weigh him first a pound of flour and then a similar amount of sugar. Alfred was about to pay when he suddenly said, 'Oh, and Mum wants some suet.'

The grocer turned to the shelf and naturally picked up the front packet, but Alfred wasn't having that. 'No, not the one on the front. Mum says you keep the oldest stock there, I'll have the one from the very back.'

The grocer looked cross. 'I'll tell you this, Alfred, if you weren't off to the Front, I'd give you a clip round the ear. The idea of me selling old stock!'

But as he reached back and got the packet Alfred

had asked for, Ginger stepped forward and said, 'I think I'd have a look in there before you hand it over.'

The grocer looked mystified and Alfred swung round. 'You mind your own business!'

'You ought to see what's in there first,' Ginger said calmly.

'Now don't you start with any of your jokes, Jack,' the grocer said, 'there's suet in here, likc you'd expect.'

'But that's not all,' Ginger said.

Alfred hastly made for the door, but Ginger had already bolted that while Alfred was buying his groceries.

The grocer, still puzzled, opened the suet packet and was astonished to find the valuable double row of pearls, packed down on top of the greaseproof wrapping which held the shredded fat. 'How did these get in here?'

'It's as big a mystery to me, as it is to you,' Alfred spluttered.

'I saw him hide them there on Saturday night, during the party,' Ginger said.

'I never did!' Alfred chimed in.

The grocer couldn't believe what he was hearing. 'And I thought Ronald had taken them.'

'But Ronald wasn't in the house long, was he? Remember, early on, I told you he'd disappeared and you searched the house for him?'

'That's right!'

'Well,' said Ginger, 'the main thing is, it wasn't Ronald's fault and you've got the pearls back. What you do with Alfred is up to you now, but I've got to be off.'

As Ginger unlocked the shop door and left, Alfred's protestations of innocence and the grocer's cries of thanks followed him into the street.

No sooner was Ginger outside, feeling rather pleased with himself, than he quickly hid in a doorway and pressed the button and was plunged back into the darkness. 'All I've got to do now is release Jack and collect Clyde.' He hastily reset the luminous figures to the right time and date to return just once more to the night of the party.

But by half-past ten there was no sign of Clyde. Worse, Jack had somehow got free and taken with him the rope which Ginger and Clyde needed to tie them together for their homeward journey.

27

Taking the plunge

Thinking Clyde had forgotten the time and must still be watching Ronald, Ginger went to the park. On the way up, there was no sign of either Ronald, Alice or Clyde and Ginger was left with little choice but to go into the park and search for him.

As Alice and Ronald met there, the duck pond seemed the best place to start, but as Ginger got closer, he was surprised to hear raised voices. Using the bushes for cover, Ginger made his way towards the noises.

He came out immediately behind the bench by the pond, the one he'd shared with Gran. Ginger parted the branches and peered out. The shouting was coming from a group of four young lads who had surrounded Clyde, and were busy hurling insults at him. One of them, a big lad, was shaking a large white goose feather at Clyde, shouting, 'Instead of hiding up here, why aren't you fighting in the army?'

'He's scared!' said another. 'Cowardy custard!'

And the others took it up as a chant.

'Poor Clyde!' Ginger murmured, wondering what he could do against four of them to rescue his mate.

'Make him take the white feather,' someone said.

'Yeah, it's the only badge he'll ever wear.'

'I got an idea,' the big one said, 'Aylesburys are covered in white feathers like he ought to be, let's chuck him in the pond with the rest of the ducks.'

For the first time, Clyde, who had held his ground and kept quiet, looked scared. 'No!' he said, backing away slightly. 'I can't swim!'

'We don't care if you drown, you'd never be missed!' the big one replied. 'Come on, lads, get him!'

Clyde wriggled and kicked, bit and scratched, but in spite of everything the lads managed to grab hold of him, two by the arms and the other two by his legs and then began to swing him backwards and forwards over the water.

Clyde pleaded with them, but that only made them worse and at last the big one shouted, 'All together on the count of three! One, two, three!'

On three, they hurled Clyde into the water. He landed amongst a patch of weed with a tremendous splash. There were loud protesting quacks from the disturbed ducks which had been sleeping on the pond and a good deal of scornful laughter from his tormentors.

Clyde surfaced, briefly spluttered, 'Help!!' before being smothered again by the weeds and disappearing deep into the muddy water.

Having torn off his boots, Ginger, with a loud, wordless, roar of anger, burst out of the bushes and ran across the path. Pushing aside the mocking youths, Ginger took a running jump into the patch of weed where he'd last seen Clyde.

Dad had often warned him how deep the pond, originally excavated as a marl hole, was but the length of time Ginger spent under water gave him a frighteningly clear idea. He thought his lungs would burst before he ever rose to the surface again! What made it worse was the slimy weed's strong tendrils which dragged at his thrashing limbs.

When he finally burst out, he struggled to tread water against the weight of his soaking clothes.

He shook the water from his nose and eyes; there was no sign of Clyde.

'Clyde! Clyde!' he shouted at the top of his voice.

But the only response came from the bank, where the four lads taunted him with high-pitched girlish cries of Clyde's name.

Then in amongst the weed, Ginger thought he caught a glimpse of Clyde's white shirt. Ginger forced his way through the broad leaves and grabbed Clyde. He rolled Clyde, semi-conscious, on to his back and, taking care to keep his head above water, started to tow him towards the shore.

He was within metres of safety when large stones, heaved at them by the youths, splashed dangerously close to them.

'Stupid idiots!' he yelled, but they simply threw more and Ginger knew, the nearer they got, the more danger he and Clyde would be in. Not only that, but he was having great difficulty keeping his own head above water, let alone Clyde's.

'There's only one thing for it!' he said. With an enormous effort, still treading water, Ginger managed to hold on to Clyde with one arm, whilst tugging away at some weed with the other. Eventually, when a long, snake-like tentacle came free, he bound it round them both, pressed the watch button and hoped for the best.

For an instant he knew how it must feel to be launched out of the water like a Trident missile. As they rose up together, the weed and water both sucked at their heels, reluctant to release them. But at last they were off, Ginger desperately clinging on to his mate's wet, slippery body.

'I won't drop you! I promise!' Ginger shouted above the roar of the wind which whipped past them.

But even as he said it, Ginger felt his grip on Clyde starting to slip, the length of weed he'd used to bind them together was unravelling and Ginger knew he wouldn't be able to hold on much longer.

Then there was a terrible splash, followed by silence. They'd arrived, but with no time to lose. They were still in the pond, the only difference was that in Ginger's time it was free of weed and there were no yobs to keep them off the bank.

With an enormous effort, Ginger hauled Clyde on to the shore, rolled him over and began giving mouth-to-mouth, just as he'd been taught in Life-saving. At first nothing, but then Clyde suddenly coughed. Ginger rolled him on his side and litres of water spewed out of Clyde.

'It's all right, mate,' Ginger said, as he slumped beside his friend, 'we're back safe and we rescued the pearls.'

'Thanks,' gasped Clyde and after he'd recovered a little, he grinned weakly and, looking at the exhausted, soaking wet figure of Ginger, he said, 'You're going to have trouble explaining the state of that unform to Mugsy.'

'And I'll have to buy him some new boots! I'll tell him what you'll have to tell your mam, we fell in the canal! But there's something else, this watch brought us back, but it won't take us anywhere again!'

Ginger held the watch in front of Clyde, who could see the face was cracked, probably from the impact of their landing, and full of water. 'It seems it wasn't waterproof after all! I just wish I'd used it once to go forward in time, instead of always going back. I would've liked a peek into the future, to see what's going to happen to me.'

'In your case,' Clyde said, 'you're probably better off not knowing!'

And Ginger knew Clyde was recovering, rapidly.

Thursday, the last day of term before the Christmas holiday, was the visit to the churchyard. From the moment they arrived and discovered the racket of council workmen's chain saws disturbing the peace as they cut down the old oak tree, nothing went well.

Even before they'd gone, Mr Lodge had been very scathing about what he'd described as, 'Nutt's Folly! This wholly fictitious account, attempting to turn Seth and Jethro into heroes!'

And on site, Mr Lodge persisted in pouring scorn on Ginger's version, by walking the whole thing through. 'And this, you say, is where the window was through which he escaped? And Seth was behind that wall, watching? And you say Jethro was shot, after his gallant shout of, "I'm for the King", right by the oak tree?'

'Yes, sir,' Ginger agreed miserably. He was sick enough about his precious watch being useless. Mugsy was already on his back because he was having to break in a new pair of boots. Ginger didn't need the rest of the class giving him a hard time too.

Suddenly a hideous, metallic, rasping noise from the chain saws rent the air and then they coughed into silence. Shortly after, the foreman walked across to Mr Lodge. 'You do history, don't you?' he asked.

'I am a history teacher, yes,' was Mr Lodge's pompous reply.

'What do you make of these then?' The foreman thrust his hand under Mr Lodge's nose. 'We just hit them with the saw, they were buried in the tree.' In his palm were several round, leaden balls.

Mr Lodge put on his know-it-all voice. 'They're almost certainly musket . . . balls . . .' The sentence died away and he stared at Ginger and then looked away.

'Told you, sir,' Ginger said very quietly, but quite loud enough for the whole class to hear.

'Of course, they'd have to be dated . . .' Mr Lodge blustered, but he knew the game was up!

When the class left to go back to school, Ginger asked permission to go straight home and Mr Lodge, who by then was glad to see the back of him, instantly agreed.

He was walking towards the gate when he saw Gran coming towards him. Since she'd seen the pearls and known they were safe, she been much calmer and less confused. And now here she was, wandering again! But when she reached the small, white, marble cherub, the one Ginger had used for the 'haunting' of Clyde, she knelt down and placed a small circlet of flowers on its head.

'So it's you who does that, Gran!' Ginger said.

Gran, who thought she was alone, jumped back, until she realised who it was. Then she smiled. 'Whenever I can. You know who it's for, don't you?' Ginger shook his head. 'It was placed here in memory of the little boy, Jethro, who the soldiers shot in the Civil War. That was how my Ronald died too and there's no grave in England for him. So, when I put the flowers here for Jethro, I'm doing it for Ronald too.'

'Come on, Gran,' Ginger said, putting an arm round her thin shoulders, 'let's go home.'

As they began to walk up Adventure Street, Gran was very quiet and Ginger felt he should break the silence. 'I never knew Grandad.'

'He died before you were born,' agreed Gran.

'Did you give in and marry Harold, the fishmonger's son, in the end?'

'I didn't! I had a lovely husband. Not the same as Ronald, but he was a very good, kind, understanding man, was my Will.'

Ginger stopped dead. 'You married Will?'

'Yes, dear. I wish you'd known him, you would have liked him.'

'Yes, Gran,' Ginger said with a secret smile, 'I think I would.'

There were two things special about Christmas that year. The first was that in the middle of Christmas lunch Gran suddenly produced the double row of pearls and presented them to Ginger's mum, her daughter, saying, 'I think it's time you had these. If I keep them, I'll only lose them and I'd like them to stay in the family.'

Ginger was astonished, but nobody else seemed to notice anything odd. Later, when he got Mum alone, he said, 'About those pearls. I thought they were stolen from my great-grandmother and that's what Gran's Great Sorrow was all about.'

Mum laughed. 'You've got a wonderful imagination, Ginger. Gran's great sorrow, indeed! I've never heard of such a thing!'

Ginger was thrilled skinny. At last he had proved to himself, if to nobody else, that he had managed to change history and for the better too, except possibly for Alfred.

Gran also gave Ginger a present. One khaki sock! 'There is another to go with it somewhere,' she apologised, 'but I just can't put my hand on it at the moment.'

He also received a present from Carter-Symes. It came with a note which said, 'I'm sorry the watch wasn't much of a present, but I've been working on Virtual Reality and I'd like you to try this out.'

'This' was a rather peculiar head-set, a cross between a pair of headphones and the hood of the kind of hair dryer Mum went under when she had a perm. Attached to it was a strange pair of binoculars and a length of electrical wire with a jointed, metal glove on the end.

Ginger was alone when he tried it on and at first nothing seemed to happen, then, after fiddling with the focus of the binocular thing, a full-colour computer representation of the sitting room he was in appeared.

The strange part was, as he stretched out the gloved hand, he knocked an ornament off the mantelpiece and weirder still, when he reached out to the settee and closed his hand round it, Ginger seemed to be able to lift it up in the air.

Just for fun he put it on the sideboard and he was concentrating so hard, he didn't hear someone come in behind him, until his father roared, at the top of his voice, 'Ginger!'

Ginger snatched off the head-set. 'What's up?' he asked.

'What is our settee doing on the sideboard?'

Ginger was about to say, 'Don't talk daft,' but when he looked, it really was . . .

Also by Ian Strachan

Wayne Loves Custard?

Wayne's on his own, temporarily separated from his parents and left to the squeaky-clean clutches of Aunt Celia and her too sanitised house. It seems like a prison sentence, but then one day in the park Wayne has a wish:

'I wish I could get to that island.'
'What's stopping you?'
'I haven't got a boat.'
'You can swim, can't you?'
'Yes, but I want to go *over* the water to get there, not in it.'

So Wayne decides to build a raft. It isn't easy; he almost gives in, but he knows he's got to get to that island. But there is also Custard. She's the sort of girl you're warned against mixing with, but much as Wayne is irritated by her, one evening in the cinema changes all that . . .

Flawed Glass

Shortlisted for the Whitbread Award

As a true islander Shona has always had a strong belief in the impossible and in magic. When her uncle leaves for America the magic seems to fade but Shona cannot stop praying for the miracle that will unlock what is stored away in a body that can hardly walk and a tongue that cannot speak. When an American businessman arrives as laird of Shona's remote island off the coast of Scotland the miracle does happen in the most unexpected way . . .

'a beautiful sensitive story . . .'
Yorkshire Post